Victoria,
   This is book 1
in my pleasure
house series!
   enjoy!
        -K-

# Guilty Pleasures

# GUILTY Pleasures

## KITTY THOMAS

*Burlesque Press*

Guilty Pleasures
© 2011 by Kitty Thomas

This book is a work of fiction. Names, characters, places, and incidents are products of the author's imagination or are used fictitiously. Any resemblance to actual events or locales or persons, living or dead, is entirely coincidental.

Printed in the United States of America

ISBN-13   978-0-9819436-6-4
ISBN-10   0-9819436-6-7

Wholesale orders can be placed through Ingram.

Published by Burlesque Press

Contact: burlesquepress@gmail.com

# Acknowledgments

Thank you to the people who supported and helped bring Guilty Pleasures into existence:

Annabel, Natasha, Claudia, and Susan: for offering critique, feedback, and copyedits.

And to M for his love and support.

# Disclaimer

This is a work of fiction, and the author does not endorse or condone any behavior done to another human being without their consent. Further, this book contains no use of condoms or talk of STDs. It is *fantasy*, not reality and should not be read in any way as resembling reality.

Warning: This book contains sexual situations of dubious consent, coercion, sexual blackmail, kidnapping, multiple partners, master/slave, girl on girl, humiliation, boot worship, oral play, and anal play.

# ONE

When will this be over? The headboard of the bed thumped against the wall in rhythm to Michael's thrusts while Vivian perfected her dead fish act. What was the saying? Close your eyes and think of England? It had been six weeks since they'd had sex. Her husband's nagging had finally pushed her over the edge.

Nothing in this interaction could be called making love. But it couldn't be called fucking either. With fucking, you at least got off. Vivian hadn't had an orgasm in two years, and even then it was acquired with her own fingers. Whoever said the thirties was a woman's sexual peak had sold her a line of shit.

A trickle of sweat from Michael's brow dripped off his face and slid between her breasts. She wondered how much time, free from his touch, this mockery of the sexual act would buy her. Vivian's shopping list scrolled through her head, a welcome distraction.

He grunted indelicately and came.

Birth control for such an infrequent joining. What a waste of money. Then again, Michael was rolling in money. He collapsed on top of her with a groan, his skin slick with sweat. She lay there, barely breathing, waiting. A couple of minutes of this pseudo-intimacy passed before he rolled off her.

"I'm going to take a shower. I'll be late for work."

She didn't bother bringing up the fact that he owned the company. Michael had a pathological need to be punctual.

He reached out to touch her again, and she couldn't stop the instinct to pull away. His answering look of contempt made her feel dirty for having had sex with her own husband.

"You're never here with me," he said.

Vivian rolled over, ignoring the accusation. He'd just had an orgasm. She hadn't, and he never seemed to care to help her with that matter. Even as she thought it, she knew she was lying to herself.

He'd made the effort, and she'd been just as unresponsive. Just as frigid. She'd pushed his fingers away from her clit, just wanting him to do what he was going to do, so they could be done with it, and she could try to forget her day had started this way.

A loud sigh came from his side of the bed, then footsteps receded to the bathroom. The door slammed. Vivian waited for the shower to start before getting up. She'd use the bathroom on the first floor, and with any luck, Michael would be out of the house by the time she got through.

She'd almost finished washing the memory of him off her body when a sharp rap sounded on the door.

"Vivi!"

She shut off the water and wrapped a towel around herself.

"What?"

"After the shit you just pulled you're really not making me breakfast, either?"

She flung the door open, the steam flowing out of the bathroom as if pre-announcing her ire. "You have some fucking nerve. You knew I wasn't in the mood."

"When are you ever in the mood?"

There were a million things she wanted to say, but she didn't know how to express how violated she felt every time he touched her. She wasn't even sure it was his fault anymore. She wasn't sure it was anyone's fault. She just couldn't come. It took too long. It was too difficult. She'd given up her own pleasure and resented her husband for not joining her and giving up his.

Though how much satisfaction he got fucking her limp, disinterested body was anybody's guess.

Instead of saying any of this, she brushed past him down the hallway to the kitchen, leaving a trail of water in her wake. "What do you want?"

"Coffee and toast is fine. An orange if we have any. I don't have time for much else. I have a meeting."

She felt his eyes on her as she took the bread from the bread box and slid two slices into the chrome toaster. The appliance made four at a time, but she couldn't bring herself to sit across a table from him. When she turned, the look in his eyes was hungry for something he hadn't gotten upstairs and wasn't about to have served to him on a plate with a cup of coffee.

Vivian turned away again to get his fruit. She had some idea of where his mind had just gone. Seven years of marriage will do that to you. He was likely picturing himself ripping the towel off her and fucking her on the kitchen island. It was a hot idea in theory, but in practice sexual fantasies weren't hot for her. She'd long given up fantasizing because she was tired of the disappointing reality.

It wasn't him. He was beautiful. His blue eyes used to make her heart beat faster. The slight dimple in his cheek had brought out her own smile. He worked out three times a week and had a golden tan. Nearly every time he stepped out of the shower she had the almost maddening urge to lick the drops of water off his body.

But that would lead to sex.

"This shit has to stop, Vivi. You act like it's a crime for me to want to have sex with my own wife."

She bristled. "You treat me like I'm your fucking property. Here to cook and clean up after you and spread my legs whenever you get the urge."

The glare in his eyes was predatory, just shy of pure evil. "I get the urge every day. More than once a day. I've pressed for sex maybe three times in the past month."

"Whatever." She put his toast and orange on a plate, poured coffee, then set the dishes on the table as hard as she could without breaking anything. The coffee sloshed around the edges of the mug.

"Are you going to clean that up?"

Vivian left the kitchen without a response and climbed the stairs, locking the bedroom door behind her. The tears she'd held back came spilling out. She bit back the sobs before they became loud enough for Michael to hear. He'd only think she was crying to get her way. He'd never understand.

She felt trapped in a marriage everyone believed was perfect. And she couldn't tell anyone they were wrong because the illusion was the only good thing she had going. She had no marketable skills, no fucking degree. He'd been Prince Charming, and she'd been in a fairy tale. She hadn't realized her happily ever after came with the strings of a gilded cage.

How had she allowed herself to become so isolated? There was no one Vivian could call family, but she'd once had friends. Before Michael had whisked her away into a socio-economic class that seemed to shut every-one but others of means out. The connections she'd forged with her husband's social circle felt shallow and claustrophobic at best.

The front door slammed, and she went to stand in front of the window, wiping the tears off her face. The next door neighbor was working in her garden, wearing an outfit that made it look like she only pretended to garden in porn. Her shorts were short, frayed denim that showed too much of her ass. And she wore a bikini top tied together with strings that looked as if they were about to come undone. Her feet were encased in the least sensible shoes it was possible for a gardener to wear.

Vivian raised the window as quietly as possible.

"Good morning, Jewel. You're up awfully early this morning," Michael said, oozing charm.

Vivian gritted her teeth as she watched the rehearsed bullshit artist and aspiring porn star. Jewel giggled. "Hello, Michael. You know I get up this early just to see you off."

He chuckled and got in the car. When the BMW left the driveway, Vivian slammed the window shut. Jewel looked up from her garden and smiled, her hand moving up in a wave. Vivian smiled and waved back.

It was hard to know if her neighbor was the most conniving slut this side of the Atlantic, or if she really was that innocent and unaware of her own glaringly loud sexuality.

The doorbell rang a few minutes later, and Vivian raised the window again. "Just a minute."

She threw on a pair of jeans and a t-shirt, pausing in front of the vanity to swipe a dab of concealer under her eyes. Maybe it wouldn't look like she'd been crying.

"Have you had breakfast yet?" Jewel said as soon as the door opened.

"No, I just made something for Michael."

"Good. I made homemade muffins, and I want you to try them." She grabbed Vivian's hand to drag her out of the house.

"I don't have shoes on."

"It's not hot out yet. You're fine. Don't be such a baby."

Vivian sighed and allowed herself to be dragged. *What the hell is wrong with me? She's not a slut. She's just a 21-year-old kid with a trust fund, having fun.*

"Do you like my new shoes? I was coming over to show you but got side-tracked by some weeds. I don't get why they keep growing in the flowers. I'm doing everything right."

"They're very cute." *Great. Keep talking so I feel like an even bigger bitch.*

They pushed past three yapping Yorkies into the kitchen. "It's my grandmother's recipe. I don't think I have it right yet, but hopefully they're edible."

The tears Vivian thought she'd managed to stifle, came pouring out again.

"Oh honey, what's wrong?"

She wiped her face quickly as if in doing so she could make Jewel forget the sudden outburst.

"Nothing. I'm fine."

The woman arched a brow but decided to let it go in favor of prying the muffins out of the pan.

"Are these fresh blueberries?" Vivian asked when she bit into one.

Jewel beamed. "Oh good, you can tell. I picked some up from the farmers' market yesterday."

The dogs had positioned themselves on the floor in front of the two women, staring and willing something to fall that they could fight over.

"Are you going to tell me why you were crying?"

Vivian waved a hand in dismissal. "Really, nothing. Michael and I had a fight."

"Oh." Jewel looked wistfully away, twirling a strand of blonde hair while she ate.

Vivian could tell from the faraway look in her eyes what she was thinking, and wondered once again if Michael was having an affair. What a thrill it must be to get away with it right under the wife's nose.

*Don't say it,* Vivian thought. But of course Jewel said it anyway.

"I wish I had a man like Michael. It's lonely having as much money as I have. Too many of the men I'm interested in just want to use me."

For a moment Vivian was stabbed with jealousy so sharp she thought it was the muffin disagreeing with her. Thinking about how much happier Michael would be with this 21-year-old smart, pretty nymphette. Someone who no doubt would come like a rocket when he looked at her, let alone touched her. Someone who didn't need to be taken care of in the pathetic way Vivian did.

"Why don't you find a man with some money?"

Jewel shrugged and slid her knife into the butter, spreading it evenly over the remaining muffin half. "They're too busy. Michael seems so devoted. That's hard to find now."

A dryer buzzed and the three dogs jerked their little heads toward the laundry room in unison.

"Oh shit! I'm going to be late for class." She jumped up and put her plate in the sink, then disappeared into the next room.

Vivian didn't bother asking why Jewel didn't have a maid. She knew why. It was the same reason she and Michael didn't. Maids were nosy.

Jewel returned, untying the bikini in a rush. Perfect, pert breasts bounced out like they'd been waiting all day to be taken for a walk. Vivian looked back at her plate and tried not to make mental comparisons while her neighbor finished dressing.

"I'm sorry to run out like this. I've just got this stupid ten am physics class, and if I'm late the bitch will lock the door on me. She seems to think I belong in fashion design or pottery. I'm pulling a high B in there. Doesn't matter to her." She slid the jeans on like fancy wrapping for candy every male on campus—and Michael—probably wanted to taste.

"It's okay. I've got errands."

"Take some muffins if you want," Jewel said, running a brush through her hair.

Vivian filled a couple of Ziplock bags and left through the back door.

*When Michael arrived home, she* was curled in a chair, reading a women's magazine that had arrived with the mail.

"What's for dinner?"

"I'm ordering take-out."

He sighed. "Vivian, you're home all day . . . "

She slammed the magazine shut with a crisp snap of pages and tossed it onto the coffee table. "And what, Michael? Are we poor? Is there some reason we need to be watching the money suddenly?"

"I just like it when you cook."

She rolled her eyes. "Was there a veiled compliment in there?"

"You know I've always liked your cooking." His voice turned softer as if begging her not to start another fight.

"And you know I never cook on manicure day."

Vivian watched his lips draw together in a disgusted line. She could practically see the cogs in his head turning, linking manicure day with one of her famous no-sex excuses, on par with the classic headache line.

He finally made a noncommittal grunt and retreated into the kitchen. A moment later he was back. "And, there's not even any coffee made."

"I'm not your slave. I don't know why you think my life revolves around serving you. It doesn't."

"Well, what does it revolve around, Vivi? Enlighten me. I'd really like to know. From what I can tell you don't do anything useful during your day at all. The least you could do is see to the house and cooking."

"That's all I'm worth to you, isn't it? Wouldn't it be much less drama for you to hire a maid and get a whore? You've got the money for it. Or would your conscience destroy the enjoyment of that since you'd be leaving me off on some corner somewhere? Or maybe you'd resent the alimony."

Michael's eyes flashed dangerously, and for one tense moment she thought pain was coming. He'd never raised a hand to her before. And yet, the thought was there, behind the surface. She could see it shining in his eyes.

He angrily reached inside his jacket pocket and retrieved a lavender card on linen paper. He thrust the rectangle at her. "Here."

"What is this?"

"It's a business card for a therapist."

"You think I'm crazy?"

"I think you're unhappy. And I *know* I am."

"Then why do I need the therapist and not you?"

His face was unreadable, but the anger still simmered beneath the surface. "Tell me, Vivi, what do I do wrong? I give you a life with all the comforts and security you need. I'm attentive. I take you out. All I ask for in return is that the woman I love not be so cold all the time."

"Do you really love me, Michael? Or do you feel obligated to me?"

He made a sweeping motion with his arm. "See? That, right there. I don't know where the hell that comes from. That, and whatever sexual hangups you've got going on, they need to be dealt with. If not with me, then with someone else because I can't go on this way."

Vivian peered closer at the card: *Dr. Lindsay Smith, licensed sex therapist.*

She crumpled the paper into a ball and threw it across the room. "You have got to be kidding me. This is all about your fucking libido?"

Michael advanced on her, pressing her against the wall. The frenzied look in his eyes made it clear something inside him had ripped apart at the seams to reveal the primal animal underneath. An animal who had no doubt been fighting and bucking in his cage for years.

"Michael, you're scaring me."

"Good," he growled. He held her arms to the wall and looked her over like prey. "You. Are. Going. Are we clear?" His stare alone could have pinned her.

"Michael . . . I . . . "

"The only acceptable answer here is yes."

Vivian nodded, too afraid of this new, unrestrained version of her husband to refuse his request. He released her wrists and went into his study, leaving her confused and more aroused than she cared to admit.

# TWO

Vivian stared up at the high-rise building, shielding her eyes from the reflective glare of the sun.

"Um . . . Miss . . . I don't have change for this large a bill," the cab driver said, leaning over the seat toward the open passenger-side window.

"Keep the change," she said, not taking her eyes off the building.

The driver peeled down the road before she had a chance to change her mind. Vivian took a fortifying breath and went to meet her doom.

As soon as the elevator opened on the tenth floor, soothing jazz drifted to her ears. The music had a hypnotic effect as it wrapped around her and pulled her off the elevator and toward the waiting office. Dr. Smith's waiting room was filled with house plants. If the world ran out of oxygen, this room would be the last safe haven.

It was empty, something she found odd for a Friday afternoon. Not even a receptionist. She thought Michael said he'd made the appointment for three thirty today. Maybe she got the dates mixed up.

She turned to leave when a deep voice stopped her. "Mrs. Delaney? You're my three thirty?"

"Yes?" She couldn't bring herself to turn back around just yet. She'd thought Lindsay Smith was a woman. Apparently not.

"Please, come on back. I apologize there was no one to greet you. My receptionist had a personal emergency."

Vivian turned and plastered a smile on her face. "Dr. Smith?"

"That's right."

The doctor stood at a little over six feet tall in a well-tailored, dark suit and exuded the calm command of a stock broker. He appeared to be in his late fifties with gray at his temples. He was in good shape, what she imagined Michael might look like in twenty years.

He smiled at her and turned to go into the inner office, clearly confident she'd follow.

She considered fleeing the building, but then she thought about the look in Michael's eyes the previous night, and the moment of terror at seeing a new side of her husband nearly unleashed on her.

When he'd pinned her against the wall like that, with that wildness peering out at her, she'd felt the faintest drop of wetness on her panties. The idea that she could have such an inappropriate reaction, after months of nearly no reaction, scared her more than the thought of him losing control.

No, she'd stay for the appointment this once. Then she'd reason with Michael. She had to at least appear to be trying to comply with his wishes if she wanted him to listen.

Dr Smith's office had lavender walls that matched the business cards. Not the first color choice she'd pick for a man, but the furniture and striking oak desk made up for any lacking masculinity in the wallpaper. The inner office had about as many plants as the waiting area. A long wall featured several orchids lined in a fastidious row.

The room had no couch, just a couple of comfortable-looking leather chairs that sat on either side of a small table with another orchid on it. She was glad for the lack of couch. She wasn't sure she could lie down to talk about her nonexistent sex life to an attractive male doctor. Especially with no one in the waiting room to act as a safety buffer. It felt too exposed.

He gestured and Vivian sat in the offered chair, smoothing down her skirt, wishing she'd worn pants.

"You seem very uncomfortable," he commented.

"You're observant. This must be why they pay you the big bucks."

He chuckled. "Your husband has already taken care of the financial arrangements. Would you like some coffee?"

"I'm fine, thank you."

He sat in the chair across from her and observed her quietly. "You're uncomfortable with the fact that I'm male, aren't you?"

Vivian looked at her hands. "I thought Lindsay was a woman."

"You wouldn't be the first patient with that initial impression."

"Maybe you should put a picture on your business card to clear up the confusion."

"Indeed." He was silent for a moment. "Mrs. Delaney, we won't speak about anything that makes you uncomfortable. We'll go at your pace."

She let out a slow breath and nodded.

He glanced down at a page of notes. "My receptionist gathered a bit of information for the appointment from your husband. He says you're unhappy with the relationship?"

Vivian balked at that, wondering how many personal details her husband had decided to divulge to a stranger over the phone. "I think Michael needs to come to therapy, too. If I'm coming to therapy." That had sounded more petulant than she'd intended.

"Perhaps we can arrange that for a future session."

He looked at his notes again, and Vivian suddenly wished she'd been the one to call and make the appointment. But she'd been stubborn.

"Why don't you start by telling me why it makes you so uncomfortable to be intimate with your husband."

She shrugged. "I don't know."

"Mrs. Delaney . . . ?"

"Really. I don't know. All I know is that every time he touches me I just want to crawl inside myself and die. If I knew why, I wouldn't be here."

"Was it like this from the beginning of the relationship?"

"No. In the beginning it was different."

"What changed? Did your husband do something?"

"I don't know. Before we got married things were fine. Then after . . . . " Her voice trailed off.

"Are you able to achieve orgasm with your husband?"

Vivian looked away and smoothed her skirt again. "No."

The doctor made a notation in the black notebook perched on his lap. "Sometimes these problems can be rooted in emotion. Do you believe he loves you?"

There was a long pause. She had to work to speak around the lump in her throat. She would not cry in front of the doctor. Absolutely not. "No," she said.

The silence hung between them, making the air feel thicker. Was he waiting for her to speak again?

After another beat, he said, "Why don't you believe your husband loves you?"

"Why would he?"

"You're a very beautiful woman."

"I'm on the wrong end of thirty-five. Beauty fades. Then what? I can't be his trophy forever. He'd do just as well with a maid and a whore."

The doctor visibly flinched at that. "You believe he feels obligated to you." He paused for only a moment before asking his next question. "Do you masturbate?"

Whoa. That was quite a subject jump. "I . . . um . . . I'm not really comfortable with that question."

"Very well. Let's broach the subject from a less personal place. Have you ever had a massage, at a spa or from a massage therapist?"

"No."

"Why not? Isn't that a normal part of routine pampering for someone of your level of affluence?"

She shrugged, feeling awkward with how close they were sitting.

As if he'd heard her thoughts, the doctor stood and retreated to his desk. He fumbled in the top draw until he came out with a card and handed it to Vivian.

"What's this?"

"Where I think you should start. You've exhibited discomfort with my gender, discomfort with your husband being intimate with you, and overall discomfort with being in touch with your own pleasure. I'd like you to make a weekly appointment for a massage. Allow yourself to feel something good for a change. Do you think you can do that for me?"

The business card was an aquamarine color with brown lettering that read, *Dome* in a blocky, modern font. In smaller letters in an elegant script underneath, it said, *spa and massage therapy*. She slipped the card into her purse.

"They accept walk-ins. No need for an appointment," he said, moving behind his desk. The doctor didn't say anything more, but began to busily shuffle through stacks of paper on his desk.

"What? Now? You want me to go now?"

He looked up as if shocked she was still in his office. "Why, yes, Mrs. Delaney."

"But it's only been twenty minutes. Don't I get a full hour?"

His eyes twinkled with amusement. "Five minutes ago you couldn't get away fast enough. Now you want forty more? Have you ever heard the term masochism?"

Was it okay for a therapist to say that? Then again, he was a sex therapist. Once a doctor asked if you masturbated, few topics were off the table.

"I only meant that I'm sure Michael paid for the full session."

"You show that card I gave you at Dome and tell them I sent you, and your first massage will be free. That sounds fair, right?"

He went back to the papers on his desk, effectively dismissing her.

Vivian, not knowing what else to do, stood and headed for the door. Her hand was on the doorknob when his voice stopped her.

"Mrs. Delaney?"

She turned, still flustered. "Yes?"

His teeth flashed bright white as he smiled at her. "You're going to lose all of your inhibitions."

*Thirty minutes later Vivian stood* outside Dome, arguing with herself on whether she should go inside. She'd never gotten a massage because the idea of being naked underneath a towel while a stranger touched her had never held much appeal.

Yet, hope flared that maybe it was such a simple matter. Maybe massage could loosen her up and free her to experience in bed what she'd experienced with Michael so long ago. Her hand trembled as she pushed open the heavy door and stepped inside.

A silver bell jingled overhead. The place was deserted just as the therapist's office had been. A warning buzzer in her brain started to sound, as if she were being led into a trap. And yet that seemed so silly. Before she could take the thought apart, a blonde woman in her twenties came out into the lobby.

"Oh, hi. Do you have an appointment? Fridays are generally for special appointments. Walk-ins are Monday through Thursday."

Vivian chided herself for being so paranoid and felt a small relief that there was a logical explanation for another seemingly empty building.

"Dr. Smith gave me this and told me to come by today." She retrieved the card from her purse. "I'll just come back next week." *Maybe.*

She felt herself blush, wondering if the receptionist would judge her for seeing a sex therapist. But the woman remained professional.

"If Dr. Smith sent you, we can work you in." The blonde led Vivian to an empty room with candles and a burbling table fountain. Eastern music played in the background.

"You can undress in here, then drape yourself with the towel." The girl pointed, indicating the cushioned table with a red button on the side. "Push that button when you're ready, and someone will be right with you."

"Thank you."

The woman smiled and left the room, closing the door behind her.

Vivian took in her surroundings. The room had a second door opposite from the one she'd been led into. Perhaps a bathroom? A flat screen television on one wall played a video with a low, calming voice talking about the spa and the various services offered by Dome.

Lucky bamboo grew in tiny pots around the room. There was an oriental-style privacy screen with a chair and large towel behind it. Thankfully there was no mirror. The staff at Dome must have realized how few women enjoyed looking at themselves naked, and how right before a massage wasn't the time to be reminded of one's imperfections. Though Michael had always told her she was perfect.

She considered walking out, still uneasy with the concept of being touched by a stranger. But she was afraid the receptionist might think her odd.

It *was* odd. The doctor was right. She was entirely too uptight for a woman in her thirties. She took a deep breath and disrobed, unsure what to do about her panties. Deciding to leave them on, she situated herself on the table. She hesitated a moment, then pressed the button.

Five minutes of tension passed before the door clicked open. Vivian lay there with her eyes shut, trying to relax. It was just a massage. Millions of women did this every day. And even liked it, if all the raving at the country club was any indication.

"You're my next appointment?" A male Eastern European accent—possibly Russian—greeted her ears. She squeezed her eyes more tightly shut. Couldn't she get a female for anything? She considered requesting a woman, but then she got a look at him.

Wavy, jet black hair fell over the best cheekbones she'd ever seen up close and in person on a man. The definition of his chest was visible through a white t-shirt. He had strong, well-defined arms, and large, yet elegant hands, like those of a concert pianist. She could see how those hands could be equally at home playing flesh draped over a massage table.

Her eyes traveled slowly back to his face. It was expectant. Waiting for something. Oh, yeah. An answer to his question.

"Yes," she managed to stammer.

"Very good. My name is Anton. I'll be taking care of you today."

The way he said it seemed like both a sinful promise and a sinister threat, causing Vivian's heart to start doing erratic things in her chest. He moved closer, and she tensed.

"Relax, my dear. Dr. Smith was correct. You are quite a closed-budded flower. We will open you." He made it sound so sexual and wrong. A warmth fluttered in her center and spread outward.

Her voice came out breathy, "You spoke to Dr. Smith?"

"Just a few moments ago. While you were getting ready for me."

She turned her head away so she could stop looking at him with helpless longing. She'd experienced testosterone overload today. Too many men near her in situations that were far too sexual for her comfort.

"You are Vivian, yes?" he said as he selected a body oil from a cart near the table. He was the king of the rhetorical question.

"Yes."

The slick oil made a sound as it coated his hands. He pulled back the towel to reveal her bare back. "Lovely," he murmured.

Vivian wasn't sure if he was admiring her skin, or if he was referring to her name. Before she could decide which, and whether or not it was appropriate, his hands were on her body, and she forgot how to think in full sentences. The strong, gentle kneading along her back caused her to, inch by inch, loosen and open to him and the pleasurable sensations he was delivering to her.

He was silent as he worked out the tension around her shoulders, and then her upper back and neck. Her arms and hands came next. Everything slowly began to unclench, starting with the muscle group he was rubbing and spreading outward as she let herself relax. Her body felt loose, liquid, suspended in a tranquil bubble of calming sensations.

Anton worked on her like this for about fifteen minutes, and then his hands began to slide lower, pushing aside the terrycloth until the towel was bunched around her thighs.

"Really, Vivian. Underwear? I'm disappointed."

She reached behind her frantically for the towel to cover herself. Now there was no question he'd crossed the boundary. Wasn't a massage therapist supposed to protect their client's modesty and comfort?

He gripped her wrist hard, not so hard to damage her, but hard enough to make her gasp in surprise at the rough contact and the menace behind it.

"Are you going to be a good girl and put your hands back where you had them?"

The threat sent an inappropriate flip of excitement through her stomach.

She couldn't twist to maneuver fully without exposing her breasts. Though she had the creeping feeling he would be seeing them soon enough anyway. A tear worked its way down her cheek as she tried to process the sudden shift of events. "Let me go. I'll scream."

"Do it. No one will hear you. The room is sound-proofed, and Janette went home after she announced your arrival. We're the only ones here."

The muscles in his arms were suddenly more than eye candy. They were evidence that he was the one with the power here, and he would have whatever he wanted from her.

"Anton, please . . . " She had the irrational belief that if she spoke his name, she'd reach something human, something that would stop him before this went too far.

"Lie back and relax. Fighting me is futile. You will lose, and I will be angry."

The options scrolled through her mind. She could call his bluff and scream, but somehow she knew he was telling her the truth about the uselessness of that choice. She could fight him, and lose, and end up with injuries. He could lose control and kill her. If he was willing to do this much, he was an unknown quantity. One she didn't want to stir up and test.

A few moments before, she'd found his appearance and touch heavenly. Would it be horrific to let him keep going? To just surrender to it? Could she say she'd come out the winner if she submitted rather than fought? Would it feel like less of a violation? Which would be worse? Would she hate herself later if she didn't fight hard enough, even though she could see how he'd closed off her hopes of escaping him?

She felt the palm of his hand press against her back until she was lying on her stomach again. He went back to the expert, innocent kneading of before and the fight ebbed out of her.

"Are you going to hurt me?" She hated how her voice sounded.

"Not unless you force me to."

A tear pricked at the corner of her eye. "Are you going to rape me?"

"No. I'm just going to touch you. I'm going to make you come for me, Vivian. I'm going to make you purr my name."

She shuddered as his words sent an involuntary spark of arousal between her legs. This was so wrong. She couldn't let this happen. She had to fight him. At least make the effort. But his hands were still rubbing her back, and she felt her body betraying her brain. Felt it as she succumbed to his talented touch.

"Please . . . Don't do this to me."

"That's enough talk, Vivian. I want you to lie there and close your eyes and feel. Dr. Smith tells me you can't achieve orgasm with your husband. I am going to fix you."

An intense shame washed through her at the way he spoke. As if molesting her on a massage table was *helping* her. What he was doing was disgusting. It was wrong. A voice in the back of her head chided her. *Wouldn't you have let him do this without a fuss if you were single? Would the question of consent have even been broached?*

"You're thinking too much," Anton said.

"How can I not?"

Her words were punctuated by his hand moving over her ass in a whispering caress. The towel slid to the floor. His fingers hooked underneath the edges of her panties as he slid them down.

She lay there bare and exposed, both too frightened and aroused by now to put up a meaningful fight.

His hands rubbed her ass in much the same way as they had her back. A soothing touch that nearly had a moan escaping her throat before she caught herself. Then his finger strayed into the cleft between her cheeks. She tensed and drew in a sharp breath.

He chuckled. "Not today, my flower. Another day. Roll onto your back."

"Just let me go." A moment of pregnant silence stretched between them as he ignored her request and waited for compliance. Finally, she did as he asked, and crossed her arms over her chest.

He stood back and surveyed her. "Don't cover yourself. I want to look at you."

She couldn't make herself obey him. It was ridiculous since her pussy was already on display. Why should she be so modest about her breasts? Her nipples had formed hard, achingly aroused points, and she could feel the moisture gathering at the apex between her thighs. What was wrong with her that this was turning her on?

Anton tugged her arms away from her body. "Look at me."

Her gaze slid self-consciously up to his. The look he gave her was so heated, she was afraid she'd combust under the power of it.

"Are you going to be a good girl for me?"

"Please . . . " she whimpered.

"The time for begging is over, Vivian. Are you going to be a good girl?"

She knew what he wanted, her verbal surrender to this violation. This violation that was at least as arousing as it was upsetting to her. She bit her lip as he held her gaze, waiting, his patience clearly capable of outlasting her defiance.

"Yes," she whispered. Her eyes drifted to the other end of the room, unable to look at him in her defeat.

Then his hands were on her breasts, stroking over the hardened peaks until he dragged another whimper from her. Vivian's legs fell open, her body unconsciously searching for something she knew he'd give her. Whether she wanted it or not.

"Don't move." He went to the sink to wash the fragrant oil from his hands and dried them on a monogrammed spa towel. She started to bring her legs back together but stopped when she saw the displeased look he gave her.

Oh, god. Why did that look fill her with so much shame? He held her gaze while he squirted lube onto his fingers.

# THREE

Atear trickled down her cheek, and Anton was immediately beside her to wipe it away. "Shhhh, Vivian. Do you not find me attractive?"

"Yes, but . . . "

"Do you not enjoy the way I've made you feel so far?"

She looked away from him. Her body strained to have the completion he could give her. The completion she hadn't felt with Michael for too long. But like this? With a stranger, under duress?

"Give in." His lubed fingers stroked the swollen and moist folds of her sex, eliciting a moan. Her hips bucked of their own accord to meet those long, expert fingers as they teased her opening.

"Please . . . " It was a breathy sigh.

"Please what?"

She knew she should say 'please stop, please don't', but suddenly the only thing she wanted was for Anton to fuck her with those gorgeous, elegant fingers. To hell with all the bullshit and protests spinning inside her brain.

He stopped touching her, and she looked up to find him watching, waiting for her to say it. A blush crept up her neck and into her cheeks.

"Please, Anton. Make me come."

A feral grin lit his face, and his fingers went back to work. Massaging, teasing, then finally plunging inside. As he penetrated her, his thumb caressed her swollen clit. Vivian's breath came faster as her body lurched and spiraled out of control. He finger-fucked her harder as she convulsed around him.

Anton retreated to the sink while she sat up and tried to cover her nakedness. She couldn't believe she'd let him . . . Well, *let* wasn't the right word. Was it?

"You may get dressed now."

She scurried behind the oriental screen flushed with embarrassment, both at what she'd just submitted to and the casual way he dismissed her now.

"You may require these." His hand, the hand whose digits had just been inside her, draped a pair of red lace panties over the panel.

She grabbed them and dressed quickly, trying not to think too hard about what had just happened. When she came around the screen he was leaning against the massage table.

Vivian smoothed her skirt down for the millionth time that day. "Are you going to let me go?"

"For now."

What did he mean *for now*? As if he had any power to bring her back here. *I'll never let him do this again.* The thought felt like a lie in her mind. Already her pussy ached from the absence of his fingers. Already she wanted to buck her hips at him in a vulgar invitation for more. She wrapped her arms around herself.

"You will make an appointment to see me every Tuesday and Thursday at three thirty. Do you understand?"

Her startled eyes rose to his. "I most certainly will not."

"That is your choice, of course. But if you don't, I will be sending your husband a carefully-edited version of this." He clicked a button, and the flat screen television switched from the spa information to a recording of her begging Anton to let her come.

She looked quickly around the room, searching for the hidden camera that had captured everything.

"Turn it off," she said, unable to stand watching her own desperation on replay.

"So then, I'll see you Tuesday?"

"Yes." If he edited the video, she'd never be able to make Michael understand what had happened and why it didn't look like rape on the screen.


*Vivian walked three blocks before* hailing a cab, not wanting to get in the back seat of someone's car while she could still feel the wetness between her thighs.

Michael's voice carried from the kitchen when she got home. "How was the therapist appointment?"

She dropped her purse on the kitchen island. "The doctor made me uncomfortable."

Michael looked up from his financial papers, concern in his eyes. "Really? Why did she . . . "

"He."

"Excuse me?"

"The doctor was male."

"Oh."

"Didn't you know the doctor was a man?"

Michael shrugged. "It never occurred to me. A friend at the club gave me the card. The doctor's name was Lindsay, and the cards were lavender. Kind of girlie. I just assumed." He laid the papers on the table, his eyes narrowing. "Did he come on to you?"

Vivian looked away as she felt her flesh heating again. "No. I just wasn't comfortable." She wasn't about to tell him about Dome and Anton.

"We'll find you another doctor," he said as if everything were settled.

Vivian crossed her arms over her chest. "No we won't. I did your thing. I tried it. I'm not going to therapy because you want sex. Get a mistress like a normal man, and leave me the fuck alone."

He arched a brow, his expression darkening. "I don't want a mistress. I want you."

"Well, you can't have me. I'm not your sex toy that you can just take off the shelf whenever it suits you."

His chair scraped out, and he advanced on her. "Do not try my patience, Vivi."

She stared him down, unwilling to let him win again. "Don't bully me, Michael."

He looked for a moment as if he would do something rash. Backhand her, maybe. Or perhaps lift her skirt and bend her over the kitchen island to take what he wanted. Like Anton had. She held her breath, half-hoping he would.

"I'm going to the gym," he said, instead.

When Michael had gone, Vivian went to take a bath in the downstairs tub. She lathered and scrubbed her skin raw, trying to erase what she'd done. No, what Anton had done. She was the victim, here.

But even as she thought it, she wasn't sure she believed it. Was she reframing this so she didn't have to feel guilty for what might be classed an affair of sorts? No, he'd planned to do what he'd done with or without her consent. He'd shown her how her avenues of escape had been shut down. Her consent didn't matter.

Was she trying to scrub his violation off, or her own internal submission to the way he'd played her nerve endings like a well-tuned instrument? She absently turned on the jets and found herself sliding down, twisting her body until the pulsing water vibrated against her clit.

Gripping the side of the tub, she pressed herself harder against the stream. Her mind drifted to Anton's hands inside the most private parts of her, fanning the flame of a desire she couldn't remember feeling before. Her breathing sped faster as she came, then sagged against the tub, waiting for the pounding in her chest to slow.

She jumped when she heard the front door and fumbled to turn off the jets, trying to get her breathing to appear normal, trying not to look like a woman who'd had her second great orgasm of the day.

The bathroom door burst open, and she threw a towel over herself. Michael looked annoyed by the display of modesty but didn't comment.

"Have you seen my cell phone? I thought I had it with me."

"Why do you need your phone for the gym?"

He rolled his eyes and shut the door behind him. A few minutes later, the front door slammed again, the car started, and she was alone.

As she climbed out of the tub, her legs trembled from the adrenaline surge of almost getting caught.

*When Michael returned, his mood* had shifted. Vivian had the momentary fear he'd taken her up on her casual challenge to take a lover, that maybe he already had one.

He kissed her cheek. "Get dressed. The little black number with the slit up the side. I'm taking you to that Japanese steakhouse you like."

Vivian took a physical step back. Things had been strained between them for months, and now he was acting like he had at the start of their relationship.

Her eyes narrowed. "Why?"

"Can't I take my wife out? You're right. You aren't my slave. I bring in very healthy money, and we don't get to spend a lot of time together doing couple things like we used to."

She was sure her face still held the wary expression. Who was this and what had he done with grumpy, sexually-frustrated Michael? Was it a ploy for sex? She wouldn't do therapy, so maybe he could seduce her by dating her?

Even if that was his aim, she wasn't sure why she should be angry about it. It just felt so mercenary and plotted-out. She'd seen glimpses of her husband in his business dealings. He was a manipulative shark, always knowing exactly how to play on the right emotion to lead his opponent down the path he wanted them on.

The trait had seemed sexy at first, but over the years her trust in him had diminished as she saw just how well he played the game of *good cop/bad cop*. Could she trust anything from him? Any declaration of love? Any gentle caress? The dinner-date-your-wife scheme was a tactic on the same level of what he played in business dealings.

She plastered the *good wife* smile on her face and decided to go along with it. Fighting him wouldn't do any good. If he was willing to be pleasant, for however long it lasted, she would accept the reprieve. And she *did* like the Japanese steakhouse.

An hour later she was dressed as he'd asked, with her hair in a dramatic upsweep. Her manicure was still fresh from the day before, and the striking red of her nails added an extra touch of sophistication. Michael stepped out from his walk-in closet, dressed sharply in Armani, his cologne wafting to Vivian's nose.

The man knew how to wear just the right amount. On the first inhalation, one wasn't sure if it was cologne, a special soap, or if he just naturally emitted such a pleasant aroma. Unlike many, he didn't take a bath it in. He used the smallest amount and let it blend with his natural, male scent.

Her heart lurched in her chest. *Stop,* she thought. She couldn't let herself love him again. Too much had come between them. She couldn't feel safe sharing the deepest parts of herself with this man.

It didn't help that she couldn't shake the belief, irrational or not, that he continued to stay with her as a financial decision to avoid losing money in a divorce or out of social obligation to a woman who'd never learned to fend for herself.

His hand cupped her elbow as he steered her toward the door. It was a possessive move, akin to how a man might place his hand on the small of a woman's back, while leading her through a crowded venue. A bolt of something she could barely remember shot through her at his touch, and she was simultaneously assaulted with sense memory of Anton's hands on her earlier that afternoon.

Michael didn't seem to notice her reaction. "Shall we go?"

Vivian nodded, not trusting her voice.

The restaurant was busy, but a reservation had been made, probably before Michael ever left the gym. She bristled at him making a reservation without so much as mentioning it or asking her opinion.

A petite Japanese woman took menus from behind the hostess stand and led them to an empty table.

A few minutes after they'd placed their order, a porcelain bottle of sake was placed on the table along with two small cups without handles. Michael had told her what they were called once before, but she couldn't remember. *Ochoko?*

When the waiter left, Michael poured the alcohol. Vivian sipped the cool, sweet liquid. *Sakura* served only top-notch sake. It was the cheaper grades of the beverage that were typically served warm. She remembered drinking it warm before she'd met Michael, back when she'd had very little money and thought it was supposed to be served that way.

He'd gently teased her the first time he'd brought her here when she'd complained about the temperature of her drink.

"Hello, Mrs. Delaney."

Vivian looked up, startled from the memory, to find Dr. Smith standing beside their table. He nodded at her husband. "Michael. It was good meeting you today."

Her husband nodded back.

Vivian's eyes narrowed. "I thought you didn't know the doctor."

"We met at the gym earlier. You know what a small world it is at the nicer clubs. He mentioned *Sakura*. I didn't realize he'd made dinner plans here as well."

Vivian rolled her eyes, not buying it for a minute. "Is this some trick to talk me into going back to therapy?"

Dr. Smith looked surprised. "You aren't coming back?"

Michael put down his cup. "Stop being so paranoid, Vivi. He mentioned it. I got the idea to bring you. I didn't think we'd run into him. I'm trying here."

Vivian wasn't convinced. It seemed too much like a set-up.

"I do apologize. I saw the two of you and decided to come by and say hello. I thought it would be rude not to." The doctor quickly excused himself.

"Vivi, I swear I didn't know he was coming here tonight."

Vivian stood from the table. "I'm going to the ladies room."

But she didn't go to the ladies room. Instead, she followed Dr. Smith to the back of the restaurant. He appeared to have come to *Sakura* alone, no wife or girl-friend on his arm. Maybe he'd met up with friends. Or maybe it really was a set-up, orchestrated by Michael to try to get her back into therapy. But if that was true, neither man had made much of an effort toward that goal.

Vivian caught up and placed a hand on the doctor's arm, causing him to slow his stride.

He looked down at her hand. "Mrs. Delaney?"

"I just need to know."

He guided her into the coat room, away from the noise and bustle of the restaurant. His eyes crinkled at the corners. "And what is it that you needed to know, Mrs. Delaney?"

She suddenly became tongue-tied, unsure how to phrase her question. The question that had been burning through her since Anton's fingers had turned her body into a raging furnace of need. "Um . . . "

He crossed his arms over his chest and regarded her, amused. He seemed to know exactly what she would ask, but enjoyed watching her struggle to find the right words.

"When you sent me to Dome, did you know?"

"Know what?"

Of course, he would make this difficult. She flushed with embarrassment. If he did know, she had to find out why. If he didn't, she owed it to every other woman who crossed the threshold of the therapist's office, to tell him.

"Did you know that Anton would touch me?"

"Yes, Mrs. Delaney. That would be in the job description of a massage therapist."

"No! I mean . . . did you know he'd touch me inappropriately?" she said, growing more flustered. What kind of person suspected such vile behavior from a doctor? Yet, he had made the recommendation.

"I did, yes."

She was speechless for a moment, not quite able to believe he'd admitted to sending her willingly to a spa to be molested. "Why would you do that to me?"

He took her arm and eased her into a corner. His large hand slid along her thigh, moving beneath the slit of her dress. "Anton lets me sample some of his ladies in exchange for sending them to him. Though normally I don't get to sample quite this soon in the process."

For the second time that day she felt the wetness soak through her panties as the doctor's lips grazed the side of her neck.

"Too soon in what process?"

He chuckled against her throat. "You'll find out soon enough, my dear."

She pushed against his chest, and was shocked when he voluntarily backed off. "Are you even a real doctor?"

"Does it matter?"

"Yes. No. I don't know." She tried to move past him, but his broad body blocked her exit. "I'll tell Michael what you've both done."

"No you won't. You'll lose him, and you know it. Your credibility will never be higher than mine, and Anton's when he shows your husband the video."

Lindsay pressed her against the wall and left a soft, lingering kiss on her neck. Vivian felt her pulse pounding at his lips. She shuddered and struggled to get away. The doctor's hand moved underneath her dress, his fingers brushing against the wetness of her panties.

"Let me go," she said.

"It doesn't feel to me like you want that. You're such a responsive little thing. Why couldn't you respond this way for your husband?" His words held no accusation, only curiosity.

Vivian squeezed her eyes shut and looked away as his hand began to grind against her heat. She was horrified to find her hips betraying her to press harder against him.

His mouth moved close to her ear. "Is it the danger you love? Is it strangers, the thrill of someone you don't know running his hands all over you? Perhaps you just need variety. The newness, the excitement."

She whimpered, her eyes meeting his, pleading with him to stop because she didn't trust her voice, or how it would sound coming out of her throat just then.

He considered her for a moment, then shook his head. "No, that's not it either. You like being under someone else's control. You get off being dominated like a bitch in heat."

Though his words were cruel, his tone was soft, soothing, nonjudgmental. Her eyes widened at that, not sure what to make of him. Not sure why she didn't scream, or try harder to get free.

"Yours is a token struggle, isn't it?"

She looked away again, unable to bear the perception in his gaze, wondering how many others like her he'd done this with, and why the idea excited her so much.

"Just let me go. Please. I can't . . . I can't take this."

"If you can tell me honestly that you don't like what I'm doing to you right now, I'll stop."

A finger slipped beneath the satin fabric of her panties to touch the yielding, soft flesh and incredible wetness. She flushed.

"Tell me something, Vivian."

Her eyes shot up to meet his at the use of her first name.

"If you were single, would you struggle?"

"Yes." She *would* struggle. Because if not for Michael and the idea that she couldn't just give in sexually to other men, she would have to struggle to avoid dealing with what could be wrong with her to be so turned on by this. Two attractive males touching her against her will, making her wet. Making her writhe for them.

Hadn't she felt the same way when Michael had let that thread of menace seep out with her?

"What's wrong with me?" Fresh tears ran down her cheeks, dripping onto her dress.

"Nothing. You're perfect. Just let yourself feel."

"What you're doing is wrong. What I'm feeling is wrong. It's just . . . it's so fucked up."

"Shhhh" His fingers had found the opening of her pussy and started to pump in and out of her in a rhythm far too pleasurable for the situation.

"Michael will come looking for me. He'll think I'm cheating."

"And aren't you?"

"No, of course not! I didn't ask for this. You won't let me go."

He took her to the edge of her orgasm, then withdrew his fingers and stepped back. There was enough space for her to maneuver past him, if he didn't step forward again to block her path.

"Do you want to go or do you want me to make you come, Vivian?"

Her voice was thready, barely above a whisper. "I want to go."

"You're such a little liar." He sucked her juices off his fingers, then turned and walked out of the coat room, leaving her shaking and unsatisfied against the wall.

# FOUR

Vivian sat silent in the car, not wanting to stir Michael up again. He'd noted how pale she was on her return from the bathroom and rushed them through dinner. He glanced over as he drove, a look of concern on his face.

She sighed. "Michael, I told you, I'm fine."

Uncertainty shone out from his eyes, but he turned his attention back to the road. "If you felt ill, you could have told me. I wouldn't have made you go out."

"You didn't make me go out. I wanted to go out. I'm fine."

Shame swamped her as she thought about the coat room and the doctor. Maybe he wasn't even a doctor. He hadn't answered her question in the affirmative.

Maybe Dr. Lindsay Smith was a woman, and that man had merely taken over her office. Maybe she only kept office hours Monday through Thursday. The lavender cards and walls, the orchids, the name. Didn't that all scream female?

The feeling between her legs intensified. All she wanted right now was an orgasm. Her eyes shifted to her husband.

On top of violating her, the doctor had gotten her revved up without satisfaction. She should have been more upset that he'd touched her but found she was upset he'd stopped. *What the fuck is wrong with me?*

Michael was right. She needed a therapist. She needed to be doped up on something that would bring her back around to something resembling sane. She couldn't enjoy sex with her own husband. Yet two handsome strangers had their hands on her in the space of a day, and like some writhing whore, she wanted to come.

She stared out the window as the lights of the city flitted past, thankful her husband had gone silent so she could think. Michael had been her first. Her only.

Did she resent him for that? Was she upset she hadn't had more experience, more lovers? Was she punishing him?

She began setting up columns in her brain. One column was labeled: *violated,* the other: *willing participant.* Under the violated column she considered Anton had intended to touch her with or without her capitulation. And he'd locked her in with him. He'd blackmailed her. There was nothing about the exchange that said consent.

And yet, hadn't he freed her to do something she might have done otherwise? In another set of circumstances? If she'd had another life? The thought made bile rise in her throat. Why was she reframing this? Was it self-preservation? What he'd done was wrong. Pure, and simple. There was no gray about it.

Anton and the doctor, or whoever the male posing as Dr. Lindsay Smith was, what they'd done was a crime. She should report them. Fuck the video.

The willing participant column stayed blank. Except for the pulsing between her legs.

When they arrived home, Michael settled her in bed and brought her a cup of hot tea with ginger. "It'll calm your stomach," he said.

She accepted the brew with a weak smile.

"I'm going to sleep in the guest bedroom, so you can get better rest."

She nodded, still feeling guilty for what had happened earlier that day. All the rationalizing in the world couldn't make her feel like she wasn't somehow cheating. After all, wasn't she going back to see Anton on Tuesday?

Her body hummed with both fear and anticipation over what might happen in that room with him. Would it be the same as today? Would it scare her more or less? Would she come just as hard anyway?

"Do you need anything else?"

She looked up to find Michael still hovering. "No. I'm fine."

"I'll be down the hall if you need me." When the door clicked shut, she brought her hand between her legs.

Vivian's mind flashed to the coat room with the doctor. His hands were so warm and solid. So smooth. And yet the smoothness didn't detract from his masculinity. Something about the softness of his hand, slippery with her juices, caused a warmth to flare out from her core.

She thought of Anton whispering threats in her ear, telling her she was powerless to resist the pleasure he would deliver. Then suddenly both Anton and the doctor were there, touching, stroking, observing her as she squirmed on the massage table, her legs spread wide for them.

The fantasy heightened when she imagined Michael standing to the side, watching. Not watching in a jealous rage, but with interest, his hand fumbling in his pants for his cock as she was used. The orgasm that followed caused her to shudder and rise off the bed.

She rolled to her side and let out a long breath. What the fuck? It was screwed up enough that she'd masturbated while thinking about Anton and the doctor, but why the hell had she brought her husband into it?

*Tuesday came out of nowhere.* After Michael left for work, Vivian took two showers and a bath. She tried on five different outfits, finally shaking herself back into reality. *This isn't a date. I'm going to this fucker to be abused so he won't humiliate me by sharing a video with Michael that will have me tossed out on the street without a penny.*

Despite the self-talk, she felt the familiar flutter in her stomach as she dressed in something sexier than she usually wore in the afternoon. She'd been bargaining with herself since nine o'clock that morning.

Beyond the morality of the situation, the only choice left was if she would let him break her and make her his victim. She'd decided she wouldn't. She'd already felt guilt and shame, as if she were both being molested and cheating at the same time.

She had to pick one of those feelings and go with it. So she picked cheating. As she gazed into the mirror, some part of her knowing she'd disconnected from reality to embrace an easier fantasy, she thought of this as dressing for her lover. She pulled her skirt down over her garter belt and stockings and slipped into a pair of fuck-me pumps.

She applied a translucent cherry-colored lip gloss to her lips and mascara to her lashes. Having convinced herself she was having an affair of her own free will, she snapped her purse shut with the lip gloss and her wallet inside, then went to Dome to see Anton.

The spa was crowded when she arrived. A flush crept up her neck at the idea of biting back moans behind one of those doors while women and the occasional man sat in the waiting area flipping through magazines.

Janette was at the front desk with a friendly smile on her face. Could the woman know what went on behind the door in Anton's little room? *You're being ridiculous. Of course she doesn't know.*

"Hi, Mrs. Delaney. You're scheduled with Anton in fifteen minutes. That'll be two hundred and twenty-five dollars."

A bit of the color drained back out of her face. She was paying him? To molest her? She covered her surprise with a manufactured coughing fit.

In response, Janette placed a bottle of imported spring water on the counter. It was cold from the mini-fridge under the desk. Vivian forced a smile, twisted off the cap, and drank. When she was finished, she pulled out her checkbook and wrote the check, her signature feeling like a pact with Satan.

A buzzer sounded and Janette picked up the phone, speaking in hushed tones. When she hung up she handed Vivian a receipt.

"That was Anton. He's running a little late with another client and said you should go to the restaurant and have a complimentary sandwich or soup. Whatever you like."

Vivian nodded numbly, with the weird, fake smile plastered to her face. She wondered if Anton had someone else in the room like her. Someone he touched against her will. Someone else he had some nasty artificial blackmail on.

It was too late for lunch but too early for dinner, and only a few tables were occupied in the spa restaurant. She wasn't terribly hungry, but she allowed them to seat her anyway, considering it a better alternative to remaining in the waiting room while her nerves became more frayed.

The restaurant was encased in glass, allowing bright sunlight to filter in from everywhere. Towering palms and ferns lined the walls, giving the sense of being outdoors in a lush jungle. A lush jungle that just happened to have a restaurant sitting in the middle of it.

"Madame, can I interest you in one of our soups? We have a very nice tomato bisque today."

"That would be fine, thank you."

The waiter handed her a menu. "It comes with half a sandwich."

She skimmed the selection and picked the turkey spinach.

He nodded once, took her menu, and departed.

Ten minutes later a plate and bowl were placed in front of her, along with a crystal glass and a chilled bottle of imported spring water. She'd just dipped her spoon in the soup when she felt a presence looming over her. Or perhaps it was the shadow that fell across the white linen tablecloth.

Anton. She put the spoon back in the bowl and stood, her heart going like a jackhammer in her chest.

"Sit," he said, his accent curling around her like a blanket.

Vivian hesitantly eased back into the chair as he slid into the seat across from her. The waiter returned with soup, sandwich, and tea for him.

After the man retreated to the kitchen, Anton said, "I ordered something for myself after I called Janette."

"Why?"

"I worked through lunch."

Vivian looked back at her bowl, unable to meet his gaze, knowing what would happen between them after they ate.

"Have I told you how lovely your hair is? It looks like a light brown until you get into sunlight. Then you've got those strands that glitter like gold," he said, his words turning gentle with the accent.

"Don't."

"Don't what? Don't eat? That's very rude, Vivian. I've worked all day. A man has to eat."

She made a choking sound. "Work. I'm sure it's been grueling."

He smiled pleasantly and bit into his sandwich.

She spoke low between clenched teeth, worried about drawing too much attention. "You know what I mean. You come out here to eat with me and compliment my hair like we're on some kind of date, when we both know what you're about."

"No, Vivian. You have no idea what I'm about."

A few moments passed in silence when he said, "You're not eating."

"I'm not hungry."

"Eat."

The look he gave her brooked no argument. She cast her eyes down at the bowl and slid the soup spoon between her lips.

"The sandwich, too."

A tear slipped from the corner of her eye and trailed off her face to land on the napkin in her lap. "Why are you doing this?"

"Feeding you?"

She tossed the napkin on the table and stood, her tolerance for the charade finally reached. "Fuck you.

Show my husband the video. I don't care. He'll believe me."

He glanced up mildly at her and took a sip of his tea. "And if he doesn't?"

"I'll figure something out."

"Don't be foolish. Sit and finish your sandwich."

She assessed him as he turned his attention to his soup. Was he bluffing?

"Let's say you show Michael the video," she said, testing the waters. "What will you get out of it? He'll probably kill you. You stand to gain nothing."

He laughed out loud. A couple of elderly women at a table a few feet away turned sharply at the sound, disdain on their faces over the audacity of the *help* dining in the spa restaurant.

"You think I'd just walk up to him?" Anton asked.

"You can't mail it. I'm home all day."

"I got his work address from Lindsay."

"Oh."

"Yes. Oh. Sit and finish."

Deflated, she sat back in the chair.

"Speaking of Lindsay, he said he saw you a few nights ago."

Her face turned so hot she knew it must be a deep crimson.

"He said he couldn't resist." Anton's gaze swept over her body, searing her. "I can understand." He finished his sandwich and drank the rest of his tea, then stood, extending his hand.

She put her palm in his, and he pulled her to him as if to embrace her. Instead, when she was close enough, he leaned toward her ear. "Do you see the man sitting across the restaurant beside that fern?"

Vivian looked and nodded, not liking the sinking sensation.

"He's a private investigator. I called him, pretending to be your husband. I said I suspected you were having an affair with a massage therapist here. He just snapped several photographs of us having lunch together. He'll put them in the mail to me later this afternoon. Your defense is looking weaker and weaker, my flower."

Vivian pulled away, shaken. She wanted to talk to the P.I., wanted to fight him for the camera. But how exactly would that go? She'd make a scene, and the spa staff would drag her off him and toss her out on her ass.

"You've got it all figured out don't you, Anton?"

"Indeed."

"How many women have you pulled this shit with?"

He just smiled and led her through the crowded lobby and into the massage room with the eastern music and the table fountain burbling away. Today the spa video was off.

"Undress," he said, after he'd locked the door.

She moved behind the screen, and he chuckled.

"Such modesty."

Vivian held her breath, wondering if he'd make her strip bare in front of him. But he turned and went to wash his hands in the sink, then selected an oil from the cart.

"I prefer the lavender oil on you," he said, conversationally as she disrobed and folded her clothing behind the screen.

And there it was. The arousal between her thighs, the dampness of her sex. It only took a few words for her body to respond to him like a lover instead of a victim.

She stood in front of him now, the towel wrapped tightly around her. A dream-like state enveloped her as she waited. For direction. To wake up. For something she couldn't put words to yet.

"I want you on your stomach today."

She swallowed around the lump in her throat and positioned herself on the table.

Anton moved behind her and made a clucking sound with his tongue. "Vivian, Vivian. No towel today. We are beyond that pretense. Are we not?"

She just whimpered as he pulled the towel away, baring her flesh to his gaze. His oiled hands came down on her, and she melted into him, biting back a moan the instant his fingers moved across her skin.

"I want to hear you moan for me. Don't hold back those lovely sounds."

Her eyes flew to his. "There are people out there." The lobby was far too close to the door for her comfort.

"And I've told you this room is completely sound-proofed."

She wasn't sure if she believed him. "I can't."

"Can't is no longer a part of your vocabulary." His fingers moved over her ass and started to slide between her legs. "Let go."

She shook her head.

"Vivian . . . This is the last time I'll ask nicely." Two thick fingers pushed inside, stretching her, sliding against her moist arousal.

She shuddered and let out a low, erotic moan.

"Good girl."

As fingers pumped, rubbing, massaging her from the inside, his other hand pressed firmly against her ass, pressing her against the table.

Today the pretense of a normal massage was gone. Though he spent a few moments on other parts of her body, loosening her up, they both knew everything centered on her sexual organs and how he'd manipulate them for her pleasure and his own twisted satisfaction.

When she started whimpering, he pulled away and retreated to the sink to wash his hands. She wondered if he was going for the lubricant again, and if he would use her ass this time. The possibility sent another tremor of fear through her.

He returned with a tube of something new. Not a massage oil or lubricant.

"What's that?"

He arched a brow at her. "Does my flower think she's in a position to be asking questions?"

Vivian dropped her head back to the table. "No."

He answered anyway. "It's an arousal cream. It will enhance the experience."

She listened as he squirted a dollop of the cream onto his fingers and massaged it into her clit. Almost immediately she felt engorged and wet, so aroused she wanted to beg him to fuck her with anything. His fingers, a dildo, his cock. She needed something inside her and didn't care what.

The moans she could barely bring herself to make only moments before, started to leave her in desperate, guttural sounds she didn't recognize.

His hands moved once again to her sex, but instead of penetrating her, or stroking her clit, he chose a less sensitive area. He massaged with expert precision the folds of her flesh, her inner and outer lips. Squeezing and pulling. Rubbing.

The feelings were so intense she couldn't be sure if it was the arousal cream, or the fact that he was touching her everywhere except the one hot-button place she needed to have petted. In her mind, her clit became a giant, throbbing sphere, engorged, huge, heavy. Within his grasp, but intentionally ignored.

He moved everywhere around it but never on it, causing nerves to fire up that she had no idea even existed. Before, she'd thought of sexual pleasure in terms of her clit, and on the rare occasions when Michael hit it just right, her g-spot. Now she felt herself awakened to nerve endings that seemed to stretch on and on, licking her flesh with a fire she'd never felt. Not with Michael. Not by her own hand even with the aid of a vibrator.

The desire Anton called from her was so strong that tears started to slide down her cheeks. But they weren't tears of the fear or shame from before. She felt her body arching off the table, her ass thrusting obscenely toward him. She pressed her mound harder into his hand, trying to get his fingers to make even the most momentary brush with that sensitive flesh that would send her over the edge into completion.

"Be a good girl, Vivian. You may only have what I allow you to have. You can't just take. Beg if you want it. Beg like a little slut, and I'll show you just how kind I can be."

Her face flamed at his words, but perhaps more at her willingness to obey them. And because the order turned her on. "Anton, please."

His free hand stroked her back as if he were petting a kitten. "Oh, you can do much better than that. Beg like a slut that wants it or I'll have to end our session here. I've got a busy roster today, and I'm already behind."

Desperation and fear drove her. "Oh, God, no. Don't stop. More. Please Anton, please let me come."

"Will you be a good slut for me if I let you have a release?"

She whimpered and nodded.

"I want to hear it."

"Yes, I'll be a good slut. Please. I'll do anything."

He chuckled. "You have no idea yet how true those words are."

She felt a cold, ribbed piece of glass sliding frantically inside her pussy, and then his fingers were finally stroking the center of her pleasure.

The orgasm went on for ages, coming fast and hard. Even when she thought she was finished and wanted to beg him to stop, one hand continued to thrust the dildo inside her while the other kept rubbing her clit in feverish circles, until she had a second orgasm riding on the back of the first.

She screamed out her release, the tears still flowing down her cheeks until finally he stopped and let her collapse on the massage table, her pussy dripping onto the soft vinyl.

# FIVE

Two and a half weeks of sessions with Anton passed before Michael noticed the deductions from their account. Vivian had made Chicken Kiev with buttered baby carrots and asparagus. She tried to play the role of the dutiful wife because her visits to Dome were feeling more and more like an affair, and less like the coerced sexual abuse it was.

Because she now looked forward to the visits.

Anton hadn't started doing anything too weird to her. He never got off. It was all about her pleasure. What he got out of it, she couldn't ascertain, but she didn't get the frightened butterflies in her stomach on Tuesday or Thursday mornings anymore. Massage days were a day she looked forward to, a day her body was held in an erotic limbo until Anton's elegant and precise hands could be on her again.

She'd almost started to see him as a lover. Almost. But he'd told her not to get attached. She wasn't the only woman he did this with, and some day she would move on. Did that mean he would get bored and release her from the blackmail? She should be happy at that prospect, but she felt nothing.

Michael had been civil with her, kind even, but he hadn't tried to touch her again. Her mind screamed with the possibilities. Did he suspect? Did he think she was cheating? Had Anton sent the pictures or the video? Surely if it had happened, her husband would have confronted her, and she'd be out on the street by now.

It was Wednesday and Michael wasn't even pretending to have a nice meal with her. Instead, he stared at the laptop screen, the click-clack of the keys piercing through the silence every few seconds as he shoveled forkfuls of food into his mouth without bothering to look at what he was eating.

"Vivian, what's this?"

She had no idea what he'd found, but the tone of his voice made her feel as if she were in a free fall. She put a bite of carrots in her mouth and chewed, trying to maintain her composure.

"What's what?"

He spun the laptop around so she could see the screen. He'd been looking at their joint bank account. He rarely paid attention to that account since most of his money went through a separate, much larger account she didn't have access to.

Her expression was perfectly blank as she looked at the screen, as if by pretending ignorance, he would go back to his Chicken Kiev and forget all about the matter.

"Twice a week withdrawals. What on earth are you spending that kind of money on? Jesus, Vivi, that's four hundred and fifty a week."

A drop in the bucket.

"We've got the money."

"That's not the point. What are you spending it on?"

There was no answer to give but the truth. The amount was too exact. Why hadn't she been smarter about it? Had she thought he'd never notice?

Had she wanted to get caught so this madness would end? She could have used the check card at the

ATM and taken out more varied amounts. Then she could have said she'd been shopping. Though that probably would have annoyed him, too.

She looked at her plate. "I've been seeing a massage therapist." As soon as the words were out of her mouth she wished she could take them back. Or rephrase them. It sounded like she was admitting to an affair. She chanced a glance up.

His eyes were cold, narrowed on her. He seemed ready to go off on his standard diatribe about money. You'd think they were starving, or even upper middle class.

"Why didn't you clear it with me, first?"

She shrugged. "I don't know. Dr. Smith sent me there. He thought massages might loosen me up." She didn't think her face could get any redder.

"You stopped seeing that therapist. You said he made you uncomfortable."

"I know." Her gaze was on her plate again, unable to bear the intensity in his eyes. Eyes that might see far too much of her.

"I'm freezing your access," he said, slamming the laptop shut.

All she could think was, *This is it. I'm out on the street. Anton will tell him everything.* All at once, her attempt at self-sabotage seemed suicidal. She wanted to drop to her knees and beg him not to, but instead she fell into the pattern that felt like normalcy between them.

Anger.

She leaped up from the table. "Fuck you, Michael. You stingy son of a bitch. Have I displeased you once in the past several weeks? Has your breakfast or dinner been late? Has your house been dirty? Have your shirts been wrinkled? You can't even accuse me of being frigid because you haven't made a move toward me."

*Why am I bringing that up? Shut up, Vivian. Shut the FUCK up. If he fucks me, he'll know something's different.*

She took her plate from the table and slammed it against the dining room wall, narrowly missing the curio cabinet. As the plate shattered, she looked at Michael in time to see his eyes turn to slits. He unfolded himself from the chair.

Vivian backed away and then bolted down the hallway, Michael on her heels in that slow, predatory walk like the villain in a horror film. So sure he'll reach his prey. The hall ended with a door that led to a half-basement. She'd get out that way and disappear for a few hours to let him cool off.

The door was locked. She twisted the knob frantically as if she could make it open with added exertion.

She turned then, her back pressed flat against the door, Michael only a few feet from her. He caged her with his hands and large body. She felt her hips arch toward his, as if this were foreplay instead of potential danger.

*Fuck. What's wrong with me?* He could have thrown her down on the ground right then and taken her from behind like an animal, and she would have orgasmed, maybe even before his pants hit the floor.

Her breath came out in shallow pants, her cheeks flushed from running. "Why is the door locked?"

He arched a brow. "I keep important business files down there."

"Since when?"

"Awhile." The word ground out between his teeth. His jaw clenched. He couldn't know she was trying to distract herself from the aching throb that had settled between her legs, making her overwhelmingly conscious of his maleness.

Anton had ignited something in her, awakened a beast that had been in slumber. Her libido had never been like this. She'd never been this desperate for release. She'd never wanted Michael more.

"What the hell has gotten into you lately, Vivi? You're not yourself."

She looked away, unable to take that penetrating stare any longer. He knew her far too well to maintain a secret of this magnitude for long.

She shrugged.

"It stops now."

A part of her snapped free, and she ached for something she couldn't put a name to, something she had no context to understand. She felt her body flushing, her breath coming in huge, heaving gasps as she tried to get control of herself. One hand still gripped the door handle, while the other clenched and unclenched at her side. It took every ounce of willpower not to launch herself at him and provoke him further.

Provoke him to what? *God, what the fuck is wrong with me?* she asked herself again. Yet the answer didn't come.

Michael stepped back, scrubbed a hand through his hair, and took a deep breath. "I'm leaving in the morning on a business trip. I'll be gone two weeks."

She released the door knob. "What? Why?" She couldn't remember the last time he'd been away. "What will I do with my access to the accounts frozen?"

"I'll have groceries delivered. If you need anything else before I return, you can call me."

"Are you having an affair?" The words tumbled out of her mouth before she'd realized they'd entered her brain.

He laughed. Not just a chuckle, or a derisive snort, but a full-on laugh.

"What's funny?"

"I can't believe you'd care if I was."

"So are you?" He hadn't tried to touch her since the last time. The morning sex.

"You're the only one I want, Vivi. And God help me for that." His eyes softened, and for a moment she thought he'd sweep her into a kiss. Instead, he took another step back. "I'm going to pack. Clean up that mess in the dining room."

She watched wordlessly as he turned and left her leaning against the basement door.


*When Vivian had picked up* the shattered china, used a carpet cleaner on the rug, vacuumed, and otherwise done what she would have after a normal dinner, she climbed the stairs to find Michael already asleep. His body sprawled across the bed as if he were sleeping off a hangover. His bags were packed and lined neatly next to the door.

Had they reversed roles? Was he the one now avoiding sex with her? Every scenario that played out in her mind revealed the same stark result. He had to know. But he couldn't know the truth of it. He had to think she was cheating on him. But how? What had she done to give it away? And why wasn't he confronting her or throwing her out of the house?

She'd thought she'd been discreet, except for the checks she'd written for the same amount every Tuesday and Thursday. Five checks. Over a thousand dollars paid to Anton to massage her in ways that weren't on offer at the average spa.

Or maybe he didn't suspect her. Maybe he was busy with his own affair. Perhaps all his time had been tied up in keeping secrets of his own. It was possible he didn't notice how disheveled she was when he came home on Tuesdays and Thursdays, how she went to extra trouble with dinner on those days, as if offering apologies for something that wasn't her fault to begin with.

But he ate the meals, grunted his approval, ran his fingers through her hair in something like affection, and then went back to work on some mysterious business activity on his laptop. He was shutting her out.

Was this what he'd felt with her while she'd pushed him to the corners of her emotional landscape for the past two years, trying to avoid intimacy because sex had lost its appeal?

Her libido was back now with a vengeance, but she didn't know the first thing about how to seduce her own husband. Would he even want her after all her rebuffs? All her dead fish acts, as she'd tried to make the sex act as unappealing to him as possible so he'd leave her the fuck alone . . . and fuck someone else?

Now that she had her wish, she found it far less satisfying than it had been in her mind when she'd fantasized about the peace she could have if he'd just leave her alone.

Vivian slipped into bed next to her husband. His hand curled possessively around her waist.

"Michael?" she whispered.

A soft snore answered her. He'd reached out for her in sleep. At least subconsciously he still wanted her. She ached to slip her hand between her legs, but she was afraid he'd wake up.

A few weeks ago, him waking to find his wife rubbing one off in their bed would have sent him into a manic frenzy, stripping off his boxers and taking advantage of the wet, waiting pussy. Now, with his behavior toward her shifting, she was too afraid of rejection, too afraid to open the Pandora's box that would reveal the sordid truth behind that $1,125 she'd spent.

She lay still in the silence of the house, listening to the clock on the wall, allowing the gentle tick to lull her to sleep as she snuggled in closer to his body.

It seemed only a few seconds had passed when morning came. Vivian squinted against the bright sunlight streaming through the window. She stretched her arm to the other side of the bed, knowing it would be empty and that the heat from his body would be long gone.

Vivian crossed to the window and closed the heavy, dark drapes, casting the room in shadow. She flopped back on the bed and slid her hand between her legs, Michael's face the only one she could see.

# SIX

Vivian stood in front of Dome, her dark glasses blocking out the sun as well as the emotion in her eyes. She'd dressed as if it were an ordinary session with Anton. Garters, heels, barely legal skirt length. He would only see the outfit for a few moments before she peeled it off behind the screen, and yet something in his imposing manner made her feel compelled to dress for him.

It was three thirty exactly. She'd given herself no time to wait. With a fortifying breath, she pushed the glass door open, entering the lush bubble of sin without a backward glance.

Janette smiled from behind the counter. "Hi, Mrs. Delaney, you're later than usual." She looked prepared to take her check, but Vivian shook her head.

"I'm afraid I can't keep my appointment today . . ."

Janette cut her off. "We require a forty-eight hour notice for cancellations or we have to charge you anyway."

"An emergency came up. I need to speak with Anton."

The receptionist eyed her, as if trying to assess whether the emergency line was honest. Then she nodded, at once emanating calm professionalism. She lifted the phone, pressed a couple of buttons, and spoke hushed words into the receiver.

When she hung up, she waved toward the massage suites. "You can go on back. He'll see you now."

"Thank you." Vivian felt her stomach seize up with every step toward that room, not knowing what he would do in light of her breaking their very illegal contract. She hadn't felt this afraid since her first visit, after knowing what would happen to her behind that thick, solid door.

"Vivian," he said, looking larger and more frightening than she remembered him.

She swallowed, her hand still on the knob, feeling like a rabbit ready to bolt. Only she couldn't do that. She had to stay and convince him to release her from this craziness. "I can't come back here anymore." She said the words so fast they seemed to be one word running and blurring together.

His eyes darkened and then narrowed. "And why would that be? You know the rules and what will happen if you stop coming here. I have more than enough video and photographic evidence to damn you."

A tear slipped from the corner of her eye and trailed down her cheek. "Please. You have to let me go. Michael froze the account. I don't have access to any more money."

"Borrow it." His voice was clipped.

"From who? How would I pay it back?"

"That's not my concern."

She slid to the ground, her back pressed against the door while sobs clawed their way out of her throat. For the first time she was thankful for the soundproofing. It seemed as if hours or days passed, but then she felt him looming over her.

Vivian looked up to see a box of tissues in his outstretched hand. She took a couple and wiped the tears away. Anton pulled her to her feet and brushed her hair back from her face with his fingertips.

"This is very stressful for you, isn't it?"

She nodded, her lip still trembling.

He looked almost apologetic. "I will accept another form of currency."

They'd been standing so close, nearly in a lover's embrace. She stepped back. "I'm sorry, what? You want me to have an affair with you so you won't tell my husband I'm having an affair with you?" Hysteria was making her ears ring, so it was possible she hadn't heard him right.

He chuckled. "I've already seen you, already touched you. What difference does it make, at this point, what else transpires between us? Don't look so stricken. You'll enjoy it. Just like you've enjoyed everything else I've done to you."

She felt the flush creeping up her neck and the wetness between her legs. The more control he took of her, the more it turned her on. Her mind sat as background noise, screaming at her, horrified by all of it. But like a drunken hedonist, she moved closer to him again, closer to the sin he held out like a bright, shiny apple.

The sin she couldn't be blamed for because she was the victim. Right? He owned her. At least on Tuesdays and Thursdays.

He watched the expressions play over her face and then frowned. "We are not becoming lovers in the sense you're thinking."

*You have no idea what I'm thinking.*

"Do not get attached to me, Vivian. What is happening between us will not happen forever."

"Because you'll get bored with me?"

"Hardly."

"Then why?" *Why am I asking like I want it to never end?* He was too attractive, smelled too good, had an accent that made her knees weaken with that deep, rounded tone. And he commanded her and played her body like an instrument only he knew how to wield with notes only he'd been given the music for.

"That's enough talk," he said. "Will you offer me the currency I ask, or are we back to threats? The threats do get tiresome, flower."

A lump had formed in her throat, and she worked to swallow around it. "What do you want from me?"

"Everything."

Her breath stopped for a minute and she had to consciously think about it to get it started back up again. "Everything, meaning?"

"The game has changed. You will come see me the same days as before. No money will exchange hands. Instead, you will do whatever I ask you to do for the hour and a half you're in this room."

"Sex?"

He couldn't have been more clear if he'd spelled it out on a billboard with bright, flashing lights. And yet, she had to hear the full confirmation that he was truly asking her to whore herself out to him. She could barely remember how this had started.

He held her gaze and nodded. "But more. When you are in this room with me, you will address me as *Sir*. Do you understand?"

The moment the word *Sir* left his mouth, the feeling between her legs turned into an unbearable ache she somehow knew only his hands, mouth, or cock could soothe away. She nodded quickly, not giving herself time to think and chicken out.

"Answer." His voice was harsher than she'd ever heard it.

Her eyes jerked up to his. "Yes, Sir." She paused a moment, then said, "What about Janette? She takes a payment from me every week. What will she think?"

"Janette thinks what she's told to think. Don't worry about what she thinks. Just sign in, and come to me. Now, put your purse down, and come here."

Vivian looked down to find she was clutching her bag in her hand, her knuckles turning white. With some difficulty, she managed to pry the thing out of her grip and place it next to the door. He held out a hand to her and she moved toward him.

Her mind spiraled into an abyss of endless questions and second-guessing. *Why am I doing this? I can still leave. He didn't lock the door. Is this really even about Michael at all? What difference will sex make at this point? Is it an affair, yet? Am I the victim if I keep making the choices? I could have worn a wire and caught him blackmailing me the second time. I could have turned him in.*

*I still can.*

Her head was spinning suddenly with the evidence of her own complicity in her demise. Which was easier? Being the victim? Or being the whore? Somehow she hadn't been able to erase either role from her psyche.

"Do you need a few minutes to think about this? At this point, it is your decision. You can walk away. There will be consequences, of course, but that is still your choice. You could even attempt to press charges against me, if you felt so compelled."

Did she want to press charges? He'd opened her up and made her body feel things again, things she'd missed so long she'd ceased recognizing the dull ache of longing that seemed to never leave the center of her chest. Until this.

"I don't know."

"What do you want, Vivian?"

"You. But it's wrong."

"Why is it wrong?"

"You're a horrible human being," she said, wondering if the question had been rhetorical and feeling foolish now that she was sure it had been.

"And you're a pure little virgin? Untouched. Unspoiled. The perfect victim? You could have left after our first meeting."

"I would have lost Michael."

"Does that matter to you?"

"Yes."

"You're making a bargain with the devil. I will ask increasingly more from you as time goes on. And you will give it to me. You might lose your soul in the process."

"I think it's a little too late for that."

"We are not a couple," he reiterated.

"I know that. I don't want to be a couple," she said, truthfully. She would never love Anton, but it didn't stop her loving his hands on her body.

"Lock the door and come with me now, or leave." He turned and crossed to the door at the other end of the room. The door she'd thought had been a bathroom.

Vivian trailed after him, equally scared and aroused both by what she was doing, as well as by what he might do. It seemed as if the ground underneath her had split apart. She felt herself crossing into another territory, one where she accepted it was her decision to follow him down this increasingly sinister rabbit hole, knowing the stove was hot, but unable to resist the burn.

Behind the door, was an office. Actually, *office* was too tame for it. It was more like a small studio apartment. On one end was the standard office set up, on the other was a full-sized bed with a plain black duvet. At its foot stood a large black trunk.

In the corner nearest to the bed was a kitchenette with the basics: microwave, sink, mini fridge, and cupboards. On the opposite end of the room, was another little door. The door stood open partway, and Vivian could see it was a bathroom. The entirety of the décor was minimalist and cold to the point of being sociopathic.

That last thought sent a chill skittering down her spine. No, this was not a man she could love, and suddenly, passion or no passion, she was happy she slept at night with Michael rather than the seductive demon in front of her.

"Dome is my business. I own the spa," he said, by way of explanation. "Sometimes I'm here late. Sometimes I just want to get away from home and have some privacy."

"Are you married?" She hadn't been able to stop the question in time.

He arched a brow as if considering whether or not to answer. "When you are with me, you do not ask questions. You obey. You address me properly. Are we clear?" He stood several feet away, and yet the power from his tone flowed over her, overwhelming her senses for a moment. She wanted to be indignant, upset, but his voice was doing increasingly fucked-up things to her body.

"Y-yes, Sir."

"Good girl."

He popped a disc into a CD player on the shelf behind the desk. A seductive bass boomed out of the speakers in a slow, rhythmic pull that made her feel an almost irresistible compulsion to move her hips. He smirked as if he'd caught her stopping her own movement.

"Strip for me, flower."

Her hands shook as they moved to the buttons of her blouse. Her hips, which she'd had to make behave only moments before, started to move with the music. Anton sat on the trunk and started working on the buttons of his own shirt, his eyes never leaving her, drinking her in.

The distance between them made her feel more exposed, so she came closer. If she was right next to him giving him a lap dance, it wouldn't be so uncomfortable.

He shook his head as she got nearer. "I said strip, not come over here and grind on me."

The harshness of his words made her feel dirty. "I'm sorry, I can't do this." Her brain had finally reconnected, after two and a half weeks of existing on an orgasm-overloaded high. She'd been like an addict. Well, she would quit. Cold turkey.

She buttoned the silk blouse, her face flaming. Her hand was on the knob when he pressed her against the door. His mouth was next to her ear.

"I'm sorry, flower. You walked into my lair. You made the choice. Until I let you go, you are mine. Perhaps you'll make a wiser decision next time." His tongue trailed over the side of her neck, and she sagged against the door, the fight leaving her.

"Anton, please, I can't do this."

He spun her to face him and wrapped a hand around her throat. In contrast to the violence of his grip, his thumb brushed gently over her cheek.

When he spoke, his voice was low, barely above a controlled whisper. "What did you call me?"

"Please . . . " Her hands moved to claw at him, desperately trying to release the pressure on her throat. "You're scaring me," she rasped.

He let go and stepped back, putting space between them. "What did I ask you to call me from now on?"

She looked at the floor, unable to meet the accusation in his gaze and afraid to let him see the anger in hers. How dare he feel accusatory toward her. She was the victim. *Who followed him into this room?* the betraying voice in her mind asked. She wasn't an idiot. She'd known what *Sir* meant, what this increasing control he wanted to take of her body meant.

It was what had featured in her darkest sexual fantasies, on the rare occasions before Anton that she'd had the energy to bring herself off. And the only fantasies in her mind since then.

She'd wanted to give him that control even though he didn't deserve it. She wanted to give that control to someone. But it couldn't be Michael. It would never be Michael.

Her hand drifted to wipe the tear strolling down her cheek. "Sir," she whispered.

"Take off your clothes."

From the tone in his voice it was clear he was no longer interested in a show. Suddenly the idea of a few moments before, peeling the clothing off her body as she danced for him, seemed much better than this cold and perfunctory removal of fabric.

She wanted to go back, rewind. Obey. But she couldn't, so she unbuttoned and removed the top, then the skirt without further resistance.

"That's enough. I like you in this. Did you wear it for me, Vivian? Even though you thought I'd never see it?"

She could feel the blush creeping into her cheeks again. "Yes, Sir." She wore a black lace bra and panties with matching stockings and garter belt. The fuck-me pumps on her feet added a full three inches to her height, but Anton was still taller.

He led her to the bed without a word and positioned her over his lap. She let out a gasp of surprise at the first blow across her ass. Several more landed in quick succession until she lost her breath, and the tears came in earnest.

Her flesh heated as his hand fell on her. She could barely stand the humiliation of being turned over his knee like some child. As if he were in the right and she were in the wrong.

His hand stroked softly over her skin. "You're angry," he said unnecessarily.

She wanted to make a smart ass remark about his amazing ability to state the obvious, but she kept her lips pressed together in a firm line. She wasn't that stupid.

"You have no reason to be angry. I made clear to you the bargain you were making. I gave you the opportunity to leave. Blackmail or no blackmail, you didn't have to walk into this room with me."

She remained silent, not trusting herself to speak, still feeling the urge to lash out at him.

His hand lifted from her, then came down in another sharp snap. "We aren't stopping until you let go of your anger."

Vivian struggled to get away, her first real attempt. She'd thought not fighting would make it go faster, but she couldn't imagine not being angry with him. He was trying to break her like a horse, and fantasy life or no fantasy life, she wasn't having it.

"Get the fuck off me, you bastard."

He released her, nudged her the tiniest bit, and she slid to the floor, crumpling in a little heap at his feet.

"I don't have time for this. I have a five o'clock."

"Someone like me?"

"Someone like you two weeks ago."

"I hate you."

He smiled down at her. "That's probably a wise emotion to have toward me."

She struggled to her feet and started toward the door where her clothing had been left. "Show Michael the tapes and photos, I don't give a shit."

He came after her, his hands encircling her wrists. "I didn't say you were leaving, just that I didn't have time for this right now." He led her to the bathroom. She tried to struggle away from him, but tottering in the too-high heels didn't give her much ability to maneuver.

Her eyes widened when they got inside the small room. A sturdy bar was installed vertically next to the tub. A pair of handcuffs lay on the floor next to it.

"Get in."

"No."

"Vivian, I am quickly losing patience. Things will go much easier for you if you obey me."

She saw the warning in his eyes and didn't want to test it. She climbed into the tub. He looped the handcuffs around the bar and secured her wrists.

"Screaming is pointless, but feel free to wear yourself out."

Anton made it to the door, then turned, a smirk sliding over his face. She shrank from him when he came back with purpose in his eyes. He ran his hand over her thigh, then slipped a finger underneath her panties and inside her, eliciting a shudder.

"Just as I thought. You're dripping wet for me." He removed the finger and left her alone in the bathroom.

# SEVEN

Two hours passed before Anton came back. He turned on the faucet in the sink and held a washcloth under it, then crouched next to Vivian to wipe it across her face. The coolness of the water felt good after all the crying she'd done.

She hadn't screamed, but she *had* worn herself out. She'd exhausted herself, leaning against the cool tile, sobbing, questioning her sanity for ever walking into that room with him. Did she think he was going to make all of her fantasies come true? A man like this?

"Do you have to use the bathroom?"

Her voice came out small. "Yes, Sir."

Anton unlocked the cuffs and helped her out of the tub. When she was on her feet, he held her wrists to the light.

"No chafing. You didn't struggle. Very good girl. I see some alone time did you good. If you behave for the rest of the evening, there will be no more punishment today."

Vivian waited for him to leave her alone in the claustrophobic room, but he didn't. Instead, he leaned against one wall and crossed his arms over his chest.

"I can't go with you standing there."

"Of course you can."

Seeing he wasn't going to make anything easy for her, she slid the panties down and sat on the seat, thankful she only had to pee.

She looked at him, opened her mouth, and then closed it again, unsure how the hell she was supposed to get a question answered when he'd already told her no questions. She didn't want to incur his wrath again.

He chuckled. "Do you have something you wish to ask me?"

"Yes, Sir."

"Ask."

Michael was out of town, but there was no reason to announce that fact. She was afraid if she admitted her husband's absence, Anton would keep her longer.

Vivian bit her lip, carefully choosing her words. "Will you let me go now? Michael will wonder where I've been."

"I'll release you when I'm ready to release you. I'm sure you'll come up with a suitably creative story to explain your whereabouts."

She sagged. It had been a long shot.

When she'd finished using the bathroom and had washed her hands, he led her back into the main section of his apartment. A tray sat on the bed with a glass of iced tea, grilled chicken, and vegetables.

"I brought you dinner from the restaurant. Eat while I finish my paperwork."

She sat on the bed and ate her meal while sneaking surreptitious glances at Anton. He really had no right to be that attractive. She wanted to ask how many women he was using like her, needed to know just how big his harem was, but she knew she wouldn't broach the question. While the pain of the earlier spanking had faded, the humiliation hadn't, and she didn't want the lesson repeated.

Vivian found herself afraid of him now. A fear she should have felt more strongly from the beginning. He sat behind a cherry desk with a laptop propped open, the screen creating an eerie blue glow across the planes of his face. A pair of stylish reading glasses perched on his nose, making him look a little too GQ for someone who had recently had her chained in his bathtub.

Although his eyes never strayed from the screen, he knew when she'd finished. "Take the tray and dishes to the restaurant kitchen."

"Dressed like this?"

He looked over the screen at her, a flicker of annoyance passing across his face. "We're alone in the building. Everyone else has gone home. And if I let you get dressed first, you might not come back."

*Damn right I wouldn't come back, Motherfucker.*

Sensing the leash on his temper loosening, she got up and took the tray out with her. The lights in the building were off with the exception of small, round bulbs set near the floor, illuminating the way like the pinpricks of light in a movie theater aisle.

She could see the crowded streets outside the glass door and moved quickly through the shadows to avoid being seen.

When she returned, the laptop was closed with the glasses folded and lying on top of it. Anton lounged on the bed, wearing a smirk and nothing else.

Vivian swallowed convulsively.

"Come here," he commanded.

She forced herself to move toward the bed, almost stumbling in the stupid shoes in her nervousness. *Real sexy, Vivian.*

He patted the bed beside him, and she sat, feeling awkward. "I've never done this with anyone else before."

"Did I give you permission to speak?"

Her panicked eyes shot to his. Why had she relaxed her guard? Stupid. "No, Sir."

He ran his fingers through her hair and around to the nape of her neck, gently kneading with one hand, then two. "Tell me Vivian, honestly. Do you intend to come back to me on Tuesday at our normally scheduled time?"

"Yes, Sir."

"Liar."

She tensed. It was a lie, but she was afraid if she told the truth, he'd never let her leave that room. She had to get free of him before she could vow never to come back.

"Lie to me again, flower, and you will regret it. Do you intend to come back to me on Tuesday?"

She was silent for a full minute until his hand tightened on the back of her neck. "No, Sir."

He laughed. "When I allow you to go home, you can make that decision. There are many days before Tuesday. You'll want to use every one of them to make sure you've chosen the proper course."

His hands moved to unhook her bra. She sat motionless as he slid the scrap of lace off her and gasped when his hungry mouth found the hollow of her throat, sucking and biting with such an intensity she couldn't stop the little moan that left her mouth.

Vivian felt his reverberating chuckle against her neck. "You'll be back," he whispered, his lips moving to her ear. "You want the things I can make you feel too much."

She was sure by now that she was finished playing with fire. Her justifications for returning over and over to Dome were weak and pathetic. *Instead of playing the victim, why can't I just own it?*

She closed her eyes and imagined herself watching the scene from a distance, observing her body, docile, compliant. Like a doll. His doll. His filthy little fuck doll. She didn't move to stroke or kiss him. She wouldn't initiate a single thing, but she'd do whatever he told her to do.

"I shouldn't go easy on you after your earlier disobedience. I warned you about me."

Her breath caught, but she didn't reply. She still wasn't totally clear on his speech rules, and warped or not, she didn't want to be the one in control. She relaxed as his hands moved to her front, arranging her, positioning her in the way he found attractive, tweaking her nipples into painful, hardened points.

And then she started crying, great heaving sobs that made her shoulders shake. It wasn't the pain of what he was physically doing to her. It was something much deeper, something inside of her that was clawing desperately to get out and had only needed the smallest of catalysts. She waited for him to mock her weakness, but instead he turned her so he could look into her eyes. She pulled away.

"Don't resist me, flower."

Slowly, Vivian turned her face back to him. She was sure if she looked in the mirror, her eyes would be stark, needing something but knowing this wasn't the right man to give it to her.

"Stand up, remove your panties, and bend over the bed with your palms flat on the surface."

"Please Sir . . . I . . . "

"This isn't a negotiation."

Was this his version of *I'll give you something to cry about?* She got off the bed and moved to obey him. The lid of the trunk creaked open. Several items were shuffled around, until it was finally shut again.

Anton moved behind her. "Look at the bed. Don't turn around."

The pain that flared across her ass was so sharp she lost the ability to breathe for a moment. It seared through her, causing every nerve ending she had to twinge reflexively. What the fuck was he hitting her with? It was long, hard, and that was all the information she could process before the pain was back again.

The second crack made her cry out.

"Say, 'Thank you, Sir. May I please have another?' after each one."

Vivian repeated the phrase, holding her body tense, waiting for the next blow.

It didn't come. Instead, Anton's hand brushed over skin, soothing the pain he'd just caused. Moments later, a warm tongue licked over the welt that had no doubt risen.

The tension eased and flowed out of her. Then another crack landed over the flesh that was now wet from his tongue. She screamed, then forced the words from her mouth. "Thank you, Sir. May I please have another?"

It seemed to go on forever, comfort and pain, until she was sobbing and could barely hold herself up. Her legs shook and her calves burned from standing in the heels.

She was crying for the pain, but also something more. She was crying for her own weakness, her pathological inability to seek out what she wanted in life. Staying with Michael though she was miserable, simply because he made her comfortable. Coming to Anton over and over and pretending it was about the blackmail. Because that made her comfortable, too, when nothing was her fault, when she was the victim.

"That was ten," he finally said.

Only ten? She thought she was going to die. How could that only be ten?

"You can relax, now."

She hadn't realized how hard her arms had worked to hold herself the way he'd wanted her. She collapsed on the bed, the tears still coming unrestrained. It seemed nothing could shut off the flow of emotion now that the dam had burst.

She wanted to ask him why? What had she done? How had she deserved that? If he wanted her to come back, this sure as hell wasn't the way to encourage it. As soon as she cleared the door, this madness was over. It had to be over.

The bed dipped next to her, and then he was stroking the burning welts and kissing them. Her face flamed as she felt her own wetness dripping down her thighs, soiling the bed.

Vivian jumped when his tongue probed inside her. A desperate mewl left her throat as he lapped up her juices. Why couldn't this be Michael? Why did it have to be this twisted fucker who was holding her mentally hostage?

His weight lifted from the bed, and she found herself on her hands and knees. She didn't bother resisting when he slid inside her. She could hear the evidence of her arousal as he fucked her, his body thrusting into hers like an animal as she knelt on the bed, open and receptive. Unwilling to be anything but his vessel in that moment.

"You've got the tightest, sweetest little cunt."

Every foul word that tripped off his tongue moved her one step closer to what she was sure would be the most shameful orgasm of her life. She gripped the sheets as her breathing became heavier.

"Be a good girl and come for me."

His wicked voice sent her over the edge as her muscles clenched around him, milking him, greedily pulling his essence into her. She didn't want to come after how he'd treated her, didn't want to think about what that said about her. But she couldn't stop the orgasm that tore through her, breaking down her ability to process anything beyond this moment.

When he'd finished, he rolled off of her, panting.

His accent was heavier when he spoke again. "Get dressed. I'll see you Tuesday."

Of all the arrogant, motherfucking . . .

In another set of circumstances, she would have thrown a shoe at him, but she'd already seen what he was willing to do to her and how little power she had to make him stop. She got dressed more quickly than she'd ever before managed, wanting nothing more than to hide her body from his view.

She didn't bother to argue about Tuesday.

"Oh, and Vivian?"

She turned, the disgust shining out from her eyes. She was beyond the ability to mask it.

"You will masturbate every day between now and then. When you do, you will think only about the feel of the cane across your ass. I'll ask when I see you. And I'll know if you're lying."

Vivian slammed the door behind her, convinced she'd never see this monster again.

*Michael had left the car* for her to drive while he was away. She sat behind the wheel of the red BMW and cried some more. Her hands were shaking so hard she couldn't get the key in the ignition. Finally, she gave up and laid her head over the steering wheel, trying to focus on breathing while she waited for her body to settle down.

*Would things have gone differently if I'd just stripped like he'd asked the first time?*

Of course not. He was an abusive monster. Now that she'd stopped shaking, she was aware of the pain of sitting. An incongruous smile curved her lips.

Pictures. Evidence.

There was no way Anton would convince Michael they were having an affair, even a kinky affair. No one would be able to look at the marks on her flesh and think that wasn't abuse. Especially if she went to Michael first with photographic evidence.

And then what? Go back to stale sex once every few weeks with a man she couldn't get off with? And the alternative? Being with someone like Anton? It wasn't worth the risk.

She dug in her purse for her cell. Michael could have called while she was out. Suddenly she needed to hear the safety of his voice. But there was only one message. Vivian was surprised to find it was from her neighbor.

"Hey, I thought maybe we could hang out since Michael's out of town. I don't have classes tomorrow, so I rented a bunch of movies and made popcorn balls. Come over, or call."

Vivian looked at the dash. It was eight thirty. She pressed the button to return the missed call.

Jewel answered on the third ring.

"I need something of greater substance than popcorn balls. Order us some Chinese?" Vivian's anxiety had spiked so high her brain was sending fake hunger signals.

"Sure. Where were you?"

"Shopping. See you in a few."

Vivian disconnected the call before Jewel could ask further questions. She got home as quickly as she could and changed clothes, including her underwear. She couldn't stand to keep on anything she'd worn for Anton.

The mirror over the whirlpool tub proved too hard to resist. Her eyes widened as she took in the dark purple marks from the cane. They would be bruises soon. She ran her fingertips over the raised welts, then flipped her cell phone open and dialed Jewel's number.

"I might be about forty more minutes. I'm going to take a quick bath."

"No problem. I'll keep your food warm."

She'd had a long bath before going to Dome, but she felt so dirty. It was an emotional kind of grime that seeped to the outside.

"What's wrong with me?" she said into the empty room. Her brain remained silent, refusing to supply an answer, despite the question ringing around for the millionth time.

Anton had humiliated her and hurt her. When he'd lain across the bed with that pompous smirk on his face, fully expecting to see her on Tuesday, she'd been so furious. But was she furious at him, or because her pussy had responded like a wind-up doll?

Most disturbing of all was the idea that he believed he held so much sway over her, she would return to him again. That the orgasm that rocked through her when she'd finally had his cock straining inside her walls, had been so amazing she'd forget or ignore the pain and humiliation he'd put her through.

Before she'd realized what she was doing, she'd pushed the button for the jets and pressed her clit against the spray. Vivian held onto the side of the tub as the pulsating water moved her toward another orgasm.

And God help her, but she was thinking of Anton and the caning when she came.


*The three yapping Yorkies greeted* Vivian when she arrived at her neighbor's house. With any luck her frenemy-turned-sanity-net would be able to distract her from thoughts of Anton and Tuesday looming on the horizon.

Jewel shooed the dogs away and ushered Vivian into the house.

"Your plate's in the kitchen. I got extra egg rolls."

"Thanks." If she put on fifteen pounds maybe she could get Anton to get rid of her. If he told her never to come back, surely she hadn't yet reached the level of stupidity to beg him to keep going.

She sat on the red leather sofa in the living room while the Yorkies became deathly still and quiet. They sat at her feet, staring at the plate on her lap. Waiting.

"Your dogs are fucking eerie."

"I know. They're shameless little beggars. You want me to lock them in the bathroom?"

An image of herself handcuffed in Anton's bathroom only a few hours before, leaped into her mind.

"No, that's okay. I'll just ignore them."

"They won't jump on you or try to eat off your plate. At least I managed to train them that well."

"What are we watching?"

"Okay, don't judge, but I've been wanting to watch this movie forever. It's about a legal secretary who gets spanked by her boss and . . . other things."

"Umm . . . "

"I said don't judge."

Vivian was sure her face was beet red. Had she been living in a bubble of denial? Was she surrounded by freaks? *If so, I'm a freak, too,* her inner voice chided.

Somehow she managed not to do or say anything to embarrass herself while the movie played. She shoveled the lo mein and egg rolls into her mouth without realizing she was eating them, her eyes glued to the screen.

When the credits rolled, Jewel sighed. "I would so be her."

"Really?" Vivian tried to look nonchalant.

"Oh yes. Do you think Michael would ever do that sort of thing with you?"

"Hell and no are the words that come to mind."

Jewel giggled, but Vivian couldn't bring herself to smile. She would have been that girl too. She was becoming that girl. Maybe she'd always been that girl.

Maybe that was why, after the initial thrill of her relationship with Michael had worn off, her libido had completely shut down, and why it woke again at the most inappropriate times, with Michael, with Anton, even with the doctor.

"Are you okay?"

Vivian looked guiltily at the other woman, unsure how much of her inner turmoil her face had telegraphed.

"Fine. Look, can we call it an early night?"

"Sure. You're sure you're okay? The movie didn't weird you out?"

Vivian shook her head. "I'm just tired. All the shopping."

Jewel looked as if she'd push the issue. She was entirely too perceptive, and Vivian worried the cogs in her neighbor's brain might start turning in a direction that would end far closer to the truth than she wanted to deal with.

# EIGHT

By Saturday, Vivian could no longer cope with the jumbled mess her mind had become, and took a trip to the bookstore to buy a journal.

She had to get out what was inside her head. Every sordid detail. Every thought. Every fantasy. If she didn't, she wouldn't have room in her brain for any normal thoughts. By Tuesday the journal was half-filled. She read what she'd written, then took a match to it and burned all the words away as if by doing so she could change her internal circuitry.

As Anton had requested, she masturbated every day while she thought about the caning. Each time it was easier to get off on the memory as she became more distanced from the emotions of the event. The fantasy became just one of many of the guilty, dark fantasies she'd indulged over the years. Much more frequently since going to Dome.

She could come in under five minutes now, though she'd developed a habit of dragging it out to make the orgasm stronger. Each time, the fantasy became more elaborate, went darker. It started with the caning, but it never ended there.

She found herself wondering how many of the things she fantasized about, Anton might actually do to her if she went back. Suddenly her world was filled with the twisted possibilities of the things he would do and the things she'd submit to, to come just a little harder.

She'd given up the idea that she wasn't going back. Whatever happened in that room, Anton would let her go when they were finished. When Michael returned, she'd end it.

Fuck the blackmail. She'd decided to leave her husband because the more she thought about the cane across her ass, the more she knew it was meant to be there and that Michael couldn't give that to her.

But she couldn't get it from Anton, either. He'd make her hurt, not just physically, but emotionally. She watched the bruises and welts fade in the mirror a little more each day as her opportunity to get damning evidence of his abuse slipped away.

A decisive peace fell over her as she saw herself taking control of her life and for once doing what she wanted, leaving her gilded cage with Michael and her warped cage with Anton for a world that was scarier, but free.

She met the reflection of her eyes steadily and applied her cherry-red lip gloss, pressing her lips together with a pop.

Not a victim.

Not a whore.

The woman who walked into Dome today would be different from the one who'd left on Thursday. This Vivian had determined to be honest and unapologetic.

She signed in at three fifteen. At three thirty her name was called and she went back to that room that made her ache so deeply she couldn't think.

Anton smiled when he saw her. "I knew you'd be here. I am rarely wrong about people."

She smiled back and crossed the floor to lay her purse on the massage table. "I'm leaving Michael."

A look of surprise fell over Anton's features, but she pressed on before he could reiterate his speech about not getting attached.

"What you've done to me is completely wrong. You should be locked up. I worry about the other women coming here, what you're doing to them. But I also wonder why they aren't reporting you, either.

"You're right. I'm not your girlfriend. My husband is out of town right now. He'll be back next Thursday. Until that time I'll see you, but then I'm done. With you and with him. I'll figure something out."

He arched a brow, his face a mixture of shock and amusement. "My flower is opening up and growing up, I see. Taking responsibility for your own decisions now? Right or wrong?"

"Yes, Sir." She put emphasis on the *Sir*, not wanting him to think her little monologue meant she wasn't going to fully submit to his every sadistic desire behind this door. She'd already decided she would. She had three or four sessions with him at most. Then she'd never see him again. He could show that shit to Michael, or post it on the Internet, or sell tickets for all she cared. She was done pretending that was why she came to him.

He'd opened something inside her. Fucked-up bastard or not, she couldn't punish him for that. But she also couldn't indefinitely submit to it. She couldn't lose the part of herself she'd just found, or have her entire personality subsumed underneath his sadism.

He chuckled and shook his head. "I don't know whether you're very brave or very stupid. I certainly don't consider you very smart."

She shrugged. "I wasn't aware I had to pass an IQ test to be your part-time sex slave."

His eyes narrowed. "I've indulged you and let you speak your mind, but take too many liberties and you'll wish you hadn't come back to the devil for a few last sins."

She lowered her eyes to the ground as a tremor went through her. "Yes, Sir."

"Did you do think about the cane when you touched yourself?"

The blush in her cheeks was all the answer he needed.

"Lock the door," he said.

She obeyed and followed him into the apartment.


*He used her as an object,* a toy. Within minutes of the second door closing behind them, he had her naked and on her knees.

"Do you know what you are to me, Vivian?" he asked, stroking her cheek absently.

"No, Sir."

"You are a series of warm holes, each of which I will take and use for my own pleasure. If you please me, I'll show you kindness and return that pleasure."

She couldn't stop the little whimper that came out of her mouth.

"Deep down, you're a filthy little slut. Aren't you, flower?"

"Yes, Sir."

"My blackmail held no further power over you and instead of enjoying your freedom and making new living arrangements, instead of taking the opportunity to report me to the authorities like a sane individual, you decided it might be fun to come back here and see just how hard I could ride you until your time was up. Do I have that right?"

She didn't look up, but imagined there must be a smirk on his face. He must be thinking she was the most perfect victim to ever walk through his door and spread her legs for him. Her entire body felt hot, flushed with a wanton desire that climbed with each mocking word that tumbled from his mouth.

"Yes, Sir."

He cupped her chin with one hand, raising her face so her eyes met his as he stroked a thumb over her lower lip. "Today I want to use this hole. Open. Show me what a good little cocksucker you can be."

Her lips parted. She wasn't sure which was wetter, her pussy, or her mouth, which had started salivating as soon as his cock prodded her lips. She inhaled the musky male aroma of him, felt herself slipping further under his control. She had the fleeting fear that letting herself go like this might mean she no longer had a choice to leave him when Michael returned.

Could he break her will so quickly? *How much fire am I playing with?* Rhetorical questions.

As his cock slid into her mouth, his hand gripping the back of her neck, trapping her there, she wondered if she'd have the strength to leave either man. Or if she was wrapping herself in yet another bubble of denial. Something to make it easier to face herself, to ease herself into the bed she'd just made.

She took him in, sucking, swirling her tongue over that impossibly soft skin. She felt the first glistening beads of pre-cum drip down her throat, and she pulled back to lick the tip of his cock, tasting him. She reached up to fondle his balls and was rewarded with a sharp intake of breath.

Then he put an end to her teasing as he started to thrust harder. She allowed her jaw to relax, knowing all he wanted from her was a passive hole at the moment.

She accepted it as he fucked her mouth, finding herself growing wetter the more coldly he used her. Whatever was wrong with her, she no longer cared as he spilled into her and down her throat.

"Swallow every drop."

Well, that was wasted speech. She'd intended on doing that anyway. It would have only been a hard order to obey if he'd denied her the pleasure of drinking him.

Anton went soft in her mouth and pulled out of her. She felt herself as a bundle of nerve endings all poised and waiting for any sensation from him. Would it be pleasure or pain? A little of both maybe?

Neither.

"Are you hungry?"

"What?"

He snapped his fingers in front of her face, no doubt to wipe away the glazed look that must be in her eyes. She looked up at him trying to think if she was hungry or not. She hadn't eaten since eleven that morning, but she wouldn't have thought of it if he hadn't asked. She was too distracted.

"Are you hungry?" he repeated, sounding agitated now.

"Yes, Sir."

"I'm going to get us some food, then."

She wanted to say, 'What about me?' but she stopped the words in time.

He looked down at her and chuckled, petting her head like a dog that had pleased him with a good trick. "Don't worry, flower, we're not finished. But I missed lunch again, and I don't have time to get into what I want to get into with you before my five o'clock. You don't have a set time to be home now. We don't have to rush."

Her stomach did a little aroused flip. Then she felt a twinge over the idea of his *five o'clock*. It wasn't jealousy but worry for the other women he saw and touched. When he left Vivian alone to get their dinner, she knew what she had to do.

Coercion wasn't consent. She may not have come undone from this; the net result may have been what she needed to move her life forward. Morality aside. But she couldn't selfishly spend the next week with Anton, while he victimized others if she could stop it. How would she live with herself if she did? This wasn't just about her.

She'd better enjoy whatever he did today, because tomorrow she had to go to the police. If not for her own sake, for the sake of the others he touched.

He was back fifteen minutes later with fruit and large salads filled with meat, veggies, and cheese. It was practically an entree.

He sat the tray down. Lines formed between his eyes as he regarded her. She tried to wipe any tell tale emotion from her face that might give away her plans to end this and him.

After a few moments he seemed to decide everything was okay.

"Come."

She started to get up to follow him, but he shook his head. "On your knees."

Vivian crawled across the floor behind him. He put his food and glass of water on the desk and hers on the floor.

"Eat."

She opened her mouth to make a smart ass remark, but seeing the stern look in his eyes made her drop her gaze back to the floor and her food. They ate quietly, and when they were both finished, he led her to the bathroom and gestured to the tub.

"Please don't chain me up. You know I'm not going anywhere." She hated that trapped feeling she'd gotten when he'd chained her and left her the last time. It was too helpless, too dependent. As much as some things he did turned her on, other things . . .

"That's not what I'm concerned about. I don't want you touching yourself while I'm gone."

"I won't. I promise."

"Get. In."

She reluctantly climbed into the tub and offered her wrists so he could cuff them to the bar. He left and returned moments later with a vibrator. "The lube is in the other room, but I'm quite sure it won't be necessary," he said.

Her face flamed as he easily slid the toy inside her. He turned it to the lowest setting, flicked off the light, and shut the door.

In the dark, windowless room, her entire universe centered now on her pussy and the pathetic vibrations that couldn't get a porn star off. All the toy could do was torture her.

It could have been two minutes, two hours, or two weeks when she heard the door open and the light switch flip. It was jolting to have the bathroom bathed in so much light all at once. She'd spent the past however long feeling like she was floating someplace between dreams and consciousness, that steady, dull vibration pushing at the edges of her sanity, making her so desperate to come, she'd do anything.

Which she was sure was exactly where Anton wanted her.

He crossed his arms over his chest and sighed while he watched her writhe around in the tub. "I can't imagine how sloppy wet that vibrator is now. I'm surprised it didn't fall out."

Her only reply was a whimper, too afraid to say the wrong thing.

"If it had, you would have been in for a lot of pain this evening." He observed her for another couple of minutes. "Did you lose your ability to speak?"

"No, Sir."

He closed the distance between them and removed the toy, then held it to her lips. "Clean it."

She obediently licked it clean, her arousal peaking further when she thought it could go no higher. She wriggled her wrists, causing the cuffs to clang against the metal bar. "Please, Sir."

He uncuffed her, then handed her a washcloth. "Clean yourself, and do not even think about trying to masturbate. Then I want you to get dressed."

A panicked tear slid down her cheek that he wasn't going to let her come. He wiped it away with his thumb.

"I like you best this way, flower. So desperate and horny you'd do anything. Everyone's gone for the day. We're going to my house where I have more toys. You can stay the night."

Vivian had been rubbing the wet cloth over her folds, trying not to linger, trying not to masturbate or buck her hips, when his words stopped her.

"Stay the night?"

"You'd like that, wouldn't you?"

"Yes, Sir." The idea of seeing his house, sleeping in his bed, and waking up with him the next morning, felt exciting. But at the same time, it would do nothing to help her actually end this when she'd intended. Was that why he was trying to draw her closer? To keep her?

He'd already said they didn't and wouldn't have a relationship. It wouldn't work. He wasn't a man she could ever love. Whatever happened tonight, tomorrow she had to go to the police.

"Let's go then."

He held her hand and guided her to his car. She was silent during the drive, unsure what to say that wouldn't somehow piss him off.

*What the fuck are you doing, Vivian? It's one thing at Dome, but going to his house? This guy is clearly short on sanity. Getting into a car with him? Have you lost your mind?*

No, she'd lost her impulse control right about the time her libido had spun out of its natural orbit. Her panties were soaked again. She wasn't in the best position to make a rational decision. Most people weren't when they were that horny, or they wouldn't make half the stupid sexual choices they made.

He must have seen fear on her face because he let one hand leave the steering wheel to stroke her thigh. "Everything will be okay, flower. You'll see."

She smiled weakly, irrationally comforted by his touch.

The drive was long, and the lights of the city soon faded to reveal countryside. As the minutes marched on, fewer cars passed. It started to feel as if only she and Anton existed.

He took her hand from where she'd been clenching it in her lap and squeezed it. "Someday you'll be glad we met and that I made you face yourself."

She looked out the window at passing pastures and cows sleeping under the moonlight. Her cell phone rang, jolting her out of the surreal head space she was in. She looked at Anton, questioning.

He released her hand. "Answer your phone."

She sucked in a breath. "Hello?"

"Hey, Baby."

"Michael!" They hadn't spoken since the night in the hallway when she'd been pressed against the basement door, hoping he would just throw her down on the ground and take her. Suddenly his voice was the best sound in the world.

"I was just calling to check in. Someone's going to come by and bring groceries tomorrow. He'll leave you about a hundred dollars in case you need anything before I get back."

She couldn't stop the tears that had started to stream down her face. Guilt for cheating? Guilt for leaving? Shame over not trusting him to believe her if she'd gone to him from the start? She didn't know.

"What's wrong, Vivi?"

"Nothing. I'm fine. I just miss you."

"I miss you, too. I'll be home soon. I love you."

"I love you, too."

After she disconnected the call, she slid the phone back into her purse and wiped her eyes with the back of her hand.

"Are you all right?"

She sniffled a little. "What do you care?" She caught herself only after the words had left her mouth and looked over, afraid that might have earned her a punishment. But he didn't seem to care about her outburst.

Anton lifted one shoulder in a half-hearted shrug. "Just making conversation. I thought you said you were leaving him."

"I am."

"Why? You just told him you loved him. Were you lying?"

"Why do you care about my personal life all of a sudden?"

"Just answer the question."

"We don't make each other happy. I'm an obligation to him, and he's not what I need."

"I don't believe you have the slightest notion what you need."

A few minutes later the car rolled up to a house big enough to qualify as a mansion. Could Dome earn him that much money?

Anton must have read something off her expression because he said, "The spa is only a small portion of my income. My real money is in something else."

Before she had time to process his response, an iron gate opened to let them in.

She and Michael lived in a very large house, but this was . . . well, it was ridiculous. No one needed this level of luxury, especially if they lived alone. Which Anton must, if he was inviting her over to have kinky sex.

Vivian imagined he must have a fully-equipped dungeon in a house that big. Maybe more than one. She shivered at the possibilities.

He helped her out of the car and led her up the front steps while her anxiety mounted higher. She didn't expect the door to open from the inside, or for a large, tall man who looked like a cross between a butler and a bouncer to be standing on the other side.

A mop of blond hair fell over the man's eyes. He looked surprised. "Isn't it a little early?"

Anton pushed Vivian inside before she had the chance to catalog her situation, before she had the chance to scream. Not that anyone could have heard her on such a large, rolling estate.

She looked back to Anton, needing reassurance that the warning bells going off in her head loudly enough to give her a headache, were just anxiety over her decision to come back when she could have been free.

His eyes held annoyance, but it wasn't directed at her. He was focused instead on the butler/bouncer. "I had to move the timetable up on this one. She's too unpredictable to control from a distance. It's not worth the risk to play the game out as usual. My instincts keep us out of prison and my instincts say, now."

"Shall I show her to her suite, then?"

Anton nodded.

# NINE

The stranger gripped Vivian's arm and led her through the mansion. She looked behind her to Anton, as if the pleading in her eyes would move a man who had obviously done this before. But he was the devil she knew.

Her heart pounded so hard she could feel it against her temples. The man led her through the entryway in front of a massive staircase, then down a long, ornately-decorated hallway and unlocked a door near the end.

The room was sparsely decorated, much like the hideaway at Dome had been. There was a full-sized bed with a black duvet. Chains hung behind it. A flat screen television was attached to the opposite wall. There was a large, black trunk at the foot of the bed. A small bathroom stood off to the side.

Vivian looked up to see a security camera near the ceiling. What the hell was this place?

The walls were a dark stone that reminded her of a dungeon. Maybe it *was* a dungeon. Her own personal dungeon. She could hear faint sounds coming from next door. Moans, whimpers, and cries of "Please, Sir".

She struggled futilely in the arms of the stranger as the adrenaline surged through her.

"That's enough," he said. "I know you need to feel like you did something to get away, but all you'll earn is punishment. We've had hundreds of girls in his house over the years. And not a single one of them has escaped us. You won't be the first."

The man's accent was local, his voice deep and strangely soothing despite the situation. The fight drained out of her and she turned to look into his eyes. Kind eyes. Too kind for this.

"Please, I don't belong here. You don't have to be like Anton. You can help me get away."

He laughed and shook his head. "You aren't the first to use that line on me, either. You may be here sooner than he normally brings them, but Anton never brings a girl to this house who doesn't belong here."

He guided her to the bed and locked the chain around her wrist. "This is just to keep you from rushing the door every time it's opened. The chain will reach to the bathroom when you need to go. We aren't complete monsters."

Her lip trembled as she stared at him. Not complete monsters? Who let the crazies out of the asylum to create *that* platitude?

After he secured her and slipped the key into his pocket, he got up to leave. "Someone will be with you in just a moment. Try to relax."

As if relaxing was an option in her life at this point.

"Anton?"

He shook his head. "No." The door clicked softly behind him and she was left with her self-recriminations.

How fucking stupid. *Why did I go back? For a few cheap thrills?* It was all fine and good that she was suddenly willing to explore her darker side, the secret needs and desires she'd pushed below the surface of her sterile, Stepford existence for the past several years. But couldn't she have left Michael and made those explorations in a safer environment? With someone who wasn't a deranged criminal?

There were kinky clubs with rules and safeties in place. She could have asked around, found someone safe to play with.

She tried to think back to earlier in the day when she'd looked in the mirror and decided she was finished playing the victim and the whore. And now? She was going to actually *be* the victim and the whore. No more playing.

"Michael, I'm so sorry," she whispered to the empty room.

He'd return, and she'd be gone. Then what? Would he ever give up searching for her? Would he make the connection? She dropped her head in her hands thinking about the journal she'd filled then burned. The only clue to her whereabouts, and she'd destroyed it.

Although the fantasy of being rescued by Michael was nice for a moment, she couldn't imagine the shame of him finding her here. Even if it was only partly her fault. Even if she hadn't asked for most of it. Maybe it was best the journal was ash, to save her from one more indignity.

She got off the bed and tested the length of the chain. The bathroom had a simple shower and tub combo, a toilet, and sink. There was nothing special or extra, nothing she could use as a weapon. Though with a chain locked around her wrist, fighting seemed pointless and only likely to make the situation worse.

Vivian returned to the room and sat on the bed, scooting against the wall. She pulled her knees to her chest and wrapped her arms around her legs as she anxiously watched the door, afraid of who might come in, and what he might do with her.

She didn't have to wait long. A few minutes passed before the door creaked open to reveal a blonde wearing a black silk robe and a delicate leather collar with a silver ring protruding from it.

"Janette?"

*Don't worry about Janette. Janette thinks what she's told to think.*

The woman shook her head. "No, sweetie. I'm her twin, Annette." Her mouth drew up in an annoyed fashion as if waiting for judgment to fall for having a rhyming name with her sister. Such a small identity difference when they already looked so much alike.

"Oh." Vivian wasn't sure what else to say. She was at least mildly comforted by the presence of another female. The woman appeared relatively healthy and not in any way traumatized.

Annette sat on the bed beside her. "I'm here to explain things and to answer any questions you may have." She stroked her fingers through Vivian's hair. Vivian flinched, then, realizing there was nothing sexual in the touch, she relaxed and let the other woman continue her ministrations.

The blonde took a deep breath and started a speech she'd probably given a hundred times at least. "You are here to be trained and sold as a piece of sexual property."

Blunt. Jaded. No bedside manner.

"No!" was the only thing Vivian could think to say. It was the correct thing to say. But she wasn't acting merely from what seemed proper. The *sold* part of the equation started a new sense of dread and unease, one more intense than she'd felt since her world had gone sideways.

"Shhhh." Annette brushed a strand of hair out of Vivian's eyes. "The man who brought you here is my master. I'm the only one he owns, the rest he trains and prepares for sale. You don't need to be afraid. He does an intensive background check on prospective buyers before they're allowed to take a girl home."

Vivian couldn't hold back the reflexive shudder. She looked at the collared woman with disgust. "How can you act as if this is okay? Anton is a monster. You don't mind that he's raping and then selling all these women into slavery? What kind of person are you?"

Annette's eyes narrowed. "Look, sweetheart, he gave you plenty of chances to escape. You kept coming back."

Vivian was quiet for a moment as she tried to picture Anton discussing her plight with the other woman. "He blackmailed me."

The blonde made a *phhpt* sound. "Oh, please. If your husband truly loved you, he would have believed you. If he didn't love you enough to even listen to your side, then why would you be with him in the first place? Easier to live a pampered existence than to forge your own path in life and take care of yourself? Face it, you want to be controlled. You want the choices taken from you so you don't have to think about whether or not you made the wrong ones."

Vivian could feel herself shattering. With everything that had happened and everything that was probably yet to come, the sting of this woman's words were what made her come apart. To either have stayed away from Anton or embrace with self-possession the way he'd awakened her body, would have been honorable. But this? This horrible limbo where she could neither accept who she was, nor deny it. That was the worst.

The tears started to fall until her shoulders were shaking with it. Annette pulled the trembling woman into her arms. "He would have let you go if there had been any indication you didn't ultimately need or want this."

Vivian pulled back and searched the other woman's eyes. "How can you know that?"

"Because he let my sister go. She's one of very few women he's been wrong about. When he touched her, she wasn't excited or turned on. She was just scared. She wasn't holding something tightly coiled inside of her like you were. He stopped, said he was sorry, and released her."

Vivian's mouth fell open. "Said he was sorry? Oh hey, I just molested you, and you didn't secretly like it? Sorry I didn't pick a more mentally fucked-up target?"

"It didn't go that far. He stopped immediately. Janette came to me and told me what happened. Even though he hadn't taken it far, she needed to talk, but she didn't want to go to the police. I began dreaming about him. He starred in every sexual fantasy from that point until I sought him out. In the end I became his because I'm the only one who came to him without coercion."

"What he's doing is still wrong." Vivian wasn't about to accept a sugar-coated retelling of this freak show.

Annette shrugged. "From this point on you'll have several trainers. My master doesn't want girls to get too emotionally attached to him, or to bond with him or anyone else like they will with the man who buys them. You'll address all men here as *Sir*. When you're sold, you will address that man as *Master* unless he wants a different title or for you to address others that way."

Even as the other woman's words repulsed Vivian, they still tripped her wires, still made her wet and aroused. No matter how many times she tried to tell herself how wrong it was, she couldn't make her body respond like a normal person.

"I want to go home," Vivian said.

Annette laughed. "No you don't."

"You said Anton would let me go."

"He gave you every chance to go. You chose not to. The choice is now out of your hands."

Vivian wiped her face with the back of her hand, angry at herself for all the tears. "I miss Michael." Michael was safe. Predictable.

"That feeling won't last. What would your husband say if he knew you'd slept with Anton? You know you've been too complicit for too long. Mourn the relationship like a death if you must, but accept that it's over."

"Why can't I just stay here? Why do I have to be sold?" The truth that she wouldn't be released was finally sinking in, but she was still bargaining, hoping for a lighter sentence.

"You need a master who can properly care for you and bond with you, perhaps even love you if you please him."

"Does your master love you?"

"Yes. I think he does."

"And do you love him?"

The smile on the blonde's face spoke of her honesty. "I do."

"What right do you, or Anton or anyone else have to dictate what I *need*? Surely there are plenty of women out there who might sign up for something like this voluntarily." Vivian had seen her fair share of websites where people did more than just play at being kinky.

"And those women will find what they need without our help."

"Help. Right. You're all a bunch of sick fucks. Especially Anton. Your *master* is a psycho." It was like she'd fallen into a cult where the order of the day was bizarre rationalizations.

Annette got off the bed then, clearly fed up. Anger and hurt warred behind her eyes as she crossed to the door and pushed a red button.

A few minutes later, the door opened to reveal Anton. Annette dropped to her knees.

"Leave us, pet," he said as his cold gaze met Vivian's.

"Yes, Master."

Annette left and Anton came in, the door shutting behind him with a heavy thud.

"I understand you haven't had the same amount of time as others to acclimate before being brought here. However, it's hurtful for her to hear you talk about me like that. If I ever hear you speak to my slave in that manner again, you might have permanent scars by the time I'm finished with you. Do you understand?"

Vivian couldn't stop the seething hatred. She knew she must be glaring daggers at him and she didn't very much care. In that moment she would prefer he kill her than break her . . . or do something as gauche as make money off her.

He blazed across the floor and took her chin in one hand, forcing her gaze to his. "I said, do you understand?"

"Yes," she replied tightly.

"So help me, Vivian. Do not try my patience. Yes, what?"

"Yes, Sir."

"Undress."

The metal cuff and chain on one wrist stopped her from getting too far with her shirt and bra. Anton took a key from his pocket and released her wrist so she could finish disrobing. When the blouse and bra were on the floor, he relocked the cuff.

Vivian stood by the bed, wrapping her arms around herself and watching him with an increasingly heightened wariness.

"Lie on your stomach, and stretch your arms over your head."

"Please, Sir. I'm sorry." Pride was a distant memory anyway. She may as well attempt begging for leniency.

"You are right now, yes. And you will be even more sorry in a few moments. You'll only make it worse if you don't submit to me."

She bit her lip and then, since there was nothing else she could do, she laid on the bed. A shuffling sound came from the trunk as he sifted through to find the implement he'd use.

The paddle had holes in it, and the sting was so intense she screamed after the first blow. He was seriously pissed. She cried and begged and squirmed, but she didn't try to get away. The only thing she knew she could do to lessen his anger was just obey and take it.

He didn't say a word and didn't command her to say anything back. He merely left her alone with her misery as he brought the paddle down, over and over. She lost count after twenty. Finally, he flung it across the room.

She jumped when the piece of wood hit the stone wall.

"Goddammit, Vivian."

She waited, more scared of him now that he seemed to have lost control of himself.

"Why did you have to come into Dome and make that little speech? Can you never keep one thought in your head to yourself? I brought you here too soon, and now it's all fucked up."

Vivian watched him from the bed, afraid to set him off again. Anton finally stopped pacing and sat beside her, running his hand over her paddle-warmed ass. His fingers slipped between her thighs.

"Soaked," he said unnecessarily.

She turned from him, too embarrassed by her physical reaction to what he'd just done. No matter how hard or how much it hurt, her body turned into a well-lubed fuck toy, ready for his, or anyone else's use.

He started to rub her back, and she allowed herself to melt into the touch.

"Tell me what you are, Vivian," he said so softly she had to strain to make out his words.

"I don't know what you want me to say."

"I want the truth."

She could feel the panic bubbling at her inability to grasp what he wanted, afraid he'd be angry that she just didn't understand what he expected her to say.

He sighed, his fingers slowly sinking into her wetness and slipping out again, drawing a shudder out of her.

"I wish I'd had more time to ease you into this. Despite what you may think of me, it wasn't and isn't my intention to traumatize you. But I'm running a business. I get paid, and you get a need met that you can't properly express yet. You know what you are, but you won't say it so I'll say it for you. You're the perfect slave, Vivian."

She knew he felt the new rush of wetness that coated his fingers, knew that she couldn't deny it to him when her traitorous body kept betraying her. But she denied it anyway.

"I don't know why I react this way, but whatever you think you know about me, you're wrong."

"Careful, Vivian. I almost broke the paddle over your ass, and there is very little stopping me from finishing the act."

She whimpered, and he went back to stroking her back. The long, careful touches soothed her in spite of everything.

"You'll probably be sold for half a million dollars," he said.

Vivian sucked in a breath. She couldn't imagine anyone spending that kind of money to own another human being. She couldn't imagine the type of screwed-up mess who would do such a thing to begin with. Her body shivered under his hand.

"That excites you, doesn't it?"

"No," she whispered, arching into his touch and fighting back a moan.

"What did I say about lying? Tell me the truth."

"I can't."

"I know it and you know it, so just do us both a favor and admit it. I'm not here to judge you. It excites you, doesn't it?"

She took a deep breath, blinking away stinging tears. "Yes, Sir."

His hand gripped her waist in a proprietary way. "Because you were meant to be owned, correct?"

"Yes, Sir."

"Are you going to be a good girl for me and your other trainers, so we can match you with an appropriate master?"

"Yes, Sir." The phrase somehow got easier to say every time she choked it out.

There was a knock on the door.

"Come in," he said.

Vivian struggled to cover herself, but Anton stilled her with his hand. It was the man who'd answered the front door. He stared openly, the look in his eyes as heated as her flesh from the paddling.

Anton chuckled. "You'll get to play with her, but not tonight. She needs to rest. This has been an upsetting day for her."

The other man nodded. He handed a glass of water and a tiny paper cup with a pill in it to Vivian, forcing her to have to sit up and expose more of herself to his view. She averted her gaze, unable to stand seeing the look in his eyes as he drank her in, no doubt imagining what he'd do to her body when he was alone with it.

Vivian held the glass and unidentified drug and turned to Anton, a fearful question in her eyes.

"It's alright, flower. It's just birth control." He brushed the hair gently away from her face. "Be a good girl, and take it for me."

She looked uncertainly once more into the paper cup, then downed the pill, chasing it with water.

The bouncer/butler took the empty cup and glass from her then stepped back but continued to stare. She could feel her face flaming from his inspection and had to fight the urge to try to use her arms to shield herself.

"She's a shy little thing, isn't she?" he commented.

"Indeed," Anton said, stroking her neck. "I don't think she's been with very many men."

She didn't think she'd ever get used to people talking about her right in front of her like she wasn't in the room. Like she was a thing, rather than a person.

He turned to her then. "Tell me, flower, how many men have seen you naked besides us?"

"Just Michael," she whispered.

"Jesus," the bouncer/butler said.

Anton chuckled. "Stop salivating, Gabe. She's scared enough as it is."

Vivian wanted to burrow her head against Anton's shoulder and hide from both of them, but he stood, leaving her exposed on the bed. He moved in front of her and helped her to her feet.

"Relax." He pulled back the covers and nudged her toward the bed again. She curled up on the mattress, and he covered her with the duvet. "Sleep now. You've got lots of new experiences tomorrow."

The two men left her with a painfully sore ass and only silence to comfort her.

# TEN

Vivian had lain in bed for thirty minutes before she threw off the covers in frustration. The chain barely reached the door. To her surprise, the knob turned easily in her hand. But with the restraining metal cuff, an unlocked door was pointless. A tease.

She flicked the light switch and pushed a button to turn on the flat screen television. Nothing happened. Was it just for show? Her gaze shifted to the security camera overhead, aimed at the bed, red light flashing. Recording her every move. She wondered if she'd be punished for this.

She opened the trunk next and wished she hadn't. Riding crops, whips, canes, floggers, paddles, nipple clamps, gags, blindfolds, ropes . . .

On one end of the room stood a chest of drawers. The drawers on one side contained lingerie, mostly corsets. The other had swimsuits, white T-shirts, and brightly-colored sporty gym shorts. The top drawer was socks and tennis shoes. Everything was in her size.

She glanced at the cracked bathroom door. She'd kill for a shower about now, if for nothing more than psychological reasons. She knew she couldn't really clean off anything that happened, but she could pretend.

No matter what Anton had made her say under duress, or how much her body agreed with him, once she'd been left alone, she had some serious fucking doubts. But that was good. Doubts made her sane.

Anton and even Gabe, were hot and took care of themselves. She could see where she might want them in some visceral, primal way. She could even understand where some part of her might want them to bend her over a counter and take her from behind.

But everything else? She shuddered and wrapped her arms protectively around herself, becoming more aware of the physical chain binding her to this location.

She let the shower run for a few seconds to get warm, then stepped into the first private and safe space she'd had since stupidly walking back into Dome.

Once under the spray, the dam burst. She cried over what she'd lost and the unknowns about her future. Would Anton keep his word and sell her to someone who would own her but not abuse her? Or not abuse her beyond the simple act of ownership? Could she be content under someone else's full command?

She thought about the way Michael had treated her like his maid and how infuriated it made her. Would she have felt differently if there had been a more sexually-dominant edge? If she hadn't felt caught in limbo between her darkest sexual fantasies and her tame and unfulfilling reality?

Vivian hissed when she turned and the water hit the still-painful globes of her ass. Her hand froze momentarily when she realized both the shampoo and soap were lavender.

When she was clean and had stopped crying, she turned off the water and dried herself. The reflective surface of the mirror over the sink beckoned to her to inspect the angry, red welts. She ran her fingertips over the marks and stared at them for a long time until she saw movement behind her and spun around.

Annette stood in the bathroom doorway, still in the black robe with the leather collar around her neck.

"What are you doing here?" Vivian wasn't feeling particularly generous toward the woman at the moment.

The blonde's eyes glistened with unshed tears, and Vivian fought to bite back a nasty remark. The other woman might push the tattletale button again.

"Vivian, I'm so sorry. Please don't be angry with me. I had to push the button. He was watching the surveillance footage, and he would have known I was upset. That was what he told me to do. I can't disobey him."

She looked like a lost little girl, her pose defensive, genuinely upset she'd done something that had led to distress for another.

Vivian sighed, the anger leaking out of her. "Don't cry. It's not like he made me bleed." She enfolded the other woman in her arms, forgetting about her nudity until the soft silk of the robe pressed against her breasts, her stomach, her thighs, her mons. The curves of her body molded against the curves of Annette, with only a thin scrap of fabric separating them.

A moment later, Annette's mouth had found and was sucking on Vivian's pulse point as her hands gently soothed the marks left by Anton's paddle.

Vivian had always noticed beautiful women and had never been repelled by a hot girl-on-girl kiss. At the same time, she'd never felt the need to explore or experiment, always assuming her heterosexuality was a settled thing.

As Annette's soft lips kissed a line from Vivian's throat to her mouth, it seemed perhaps the issue of her orientation was more flexible than she'd wanted to admit. She opened her mouth under the warm, insistent tongue, and felt the first flames of arousal as the other woman let out a strangled whimper against her.

She could taste Annette's strawberry lip gloss and wanted to eat it right off her mouth. Instead, she gently gripped the woman's arms and led her back to the bedroom. She fumbled with the tie of Annette's robe, and soon the blonde's ample breasts were tumbling out, thrusting into Vivian's waiting hands.

"Wait," Vivian said.

"What's wrong?" Annette looked self-conscious, having come back to herself. "I'm sorry. I thought you wanted . . . "

Vivian shook her head and pointed at the camera. "It's not that. What about Anton? Will we get in trouble?" She couldn't believe those words had just come out of her mouth, as if she were a child waiting for a scolding for taking a cookie from the jar before dinner.

Annette grinned. "He lets me play with any of the girls I want to, as long as they want to." She glanced back at the camera. "He likes to watch. And it gives him something hot to show prospective buyers."

A bolt of lust shot through Vivian at the idea of Anton sitting in his bedroom or a private office somewhere else in the mansion, watching the security cameras and jerking himself to the sight of her and Annette in bed together. A mewling sound slipped past her lips at the thought of Gabe, and perhaps even Lindsay watching the performance as well.

Her face burned at the memory of the doctor in the coat room at *Sakura*. She'd masturbated to the fantasy of letting him finish bringing her off more times than she cared to admit.

She jumped as feminine fingers explored between her legs.

"You do want to play with me, don't you, Vivian? I can make you feel good."

She looked into Annette's eyes and threaded her fingers through her hair. The blonde was so sweet and soft. So pliant and submissive, even with Vivian. It was hard to imagine such a woman would have the nerve to approach Anton at Dome, knowing what he was and what he did, and just offering herself to him to do with as he wished. She was a hell of a lot braver than Vivian.

In answer to the question, she led Annette to the bed.

"I've never really . . . with a woman . . . I don't know what to do."

A giggle escaped Annette's mouth. It was the best sound Vivian had heard all day, and she found herself utterly charmed by the woman, no longer upset over the red button.

Annette pushed her gently back on the bed and urged her legs apart. "I'll do to you what I like done to me, and then you can do it. Okay?"

Vivian nodded and allowed herself to relax against the pillows. Annette bent over her, her long hair falling forward, teasing the already hardened peaks of Vivian's breasts. Her mouth followed, taking hold of one nipple and sucking it into her mouth. With her other hand, she fondled Vivian between her legs.

Vivian let out a gasp. She'd never experienced a sexual encounter so gentle that was still so satisfying. The constant red blinking on the camera seemed to match the rhythm of the throbbing in her pussy. Her eyes remained trained on the lens, staring out at Anton and whoever else was watching the show as she arched her back in response to Annette's teasing.

Then the woman buried her head between Vivian's legs. She jerked at the first experimental flick of tongue against flesh and found her hands reaching down to pet Annette's golden hair, urging her on. The blonde whimpered at the stroking and lapped at the bundle of nerves, occasionally plunging her tongue inside, probing and fucking her with it.

Vivian clenched at the sheets, the chain on her wrist making a light tinkling sound each time she jerked against the other woman's mouth. She felt herself coming undone and screamed her release, uncaring of who might come through the door at the sound.

Annette lapped even more diligently, wringing every ripple of orgasmic pleasure she could from her, and at the same time, thoroughly cleaning the wet mess Vivian's body had created in response to such a talented tongue.

"Stop, I can't take anymore. Stop."

The blonde laughed and got off her. "The men will make you come until they're tired of manipulating your body. Fair warning."

Vivian felt a faint tremor at that, unsure if the shudder was from fear or excitement. And unsure she wanted to know.

Annette stretched out on the bed beside her, a question in her eyes. She didn't have to hear the words to know the blonde wondered if Vivian—now sexually sated—was still interested in further exploration.

In response, Vivian straddled her, starkly aware of how her ass was on display for the camera. Not sure what got into her, she spread her legs a bit more to give the men a better view of what was between her thighs.

Annette's pussy glistened wet, already slick and ready. Vivian slid a finger inside and withdrew it to experimentally lick the digit, moaning softly at the taste of her. Annette bucked against the air, impatient for her to continue.

"More?" Vivian said, teasing and gaining more confidence.

"Yes, please."

Vivian moved lower, inhaling the musky aroma of arousal. Then she went down on another woman for the first time.

*Vivian woke the next morning* to moaning and heavy breathing. She thought at first other people were there, but when she sat up and rubbed her eyes, she found the room empty. The sounds were coming from the TV.

On the screen with a perfect color picture, was an image of her and Annette. Watching herself with the other woman, shamelessly thrusting her ass at the camera, performing, made her wet again.

The idea that Anton was going to show this video to *prospective buyers* only served to make her hotter. She spread her legs and slid her hand under the covers. The door slammed open, making her jump guiltily.

Gabe stepped into the room, six feet of tanned blond Adonis, and looked at her with a knowing smirk. His green eyes sparkled with more than a hint of amusement. "You dirty little slut. Are we going to have to make you sleep in a chastity belt? It'll mean you have to wait for one of us to take you to the bathroom. A chore we all find tedious, I assure you."

"No, Sir."

"Get up."

She was naked under the covers and though he'd seen it all, and probably her first foray into lesbian porn the night before, she found herself still shy and unable to obey him.

"I will flog you if necessary. You can start the morning with pain or pleasure. Your call. Your only choices in this house are to obey the first time, every time, or to be punished and then obey."

Her hand shook a little as she pulled back the duvet and climbed out of bed. She crossed her arms over her chest and looked at the ground.

He'd closed the door, but hadn't moved closer to her yet. She was reminded of when Anton had asked her to strip, how uncomfortable she was being exposed in such vulnerability without the other person's physical closeness. Without the intimacy.

She remained silent, unable to look at him as he continued.

"From this point on, when I or any other male walks into this room, you will immediately leave the bed or stop whatever you're doing, crawl to him, and kiss his boots. Then you will kneel at his feet and wait for further instruction."

The bottom dropped out of her stomach, and she wanted to find a hole to bury herself in, some small space to shield her from the scrutiny she knew was on her. Something that would tamp down the desire welling from within. Was this really happening? Perhaps she was only having a long and vivid erotic dream.

"Do you understand?"

"Yes, Sir."

There was a long beat of silence. A silence so loud, it hummed and almost turned into its own sound.

"Well?" he demanded, as if she really were the stupidest female he'd ever encountered.

She looked up to see the impatience behind his eyes.

"Now," he said, his tone turning harsher.

She dropped to the floor feeling as graceful as a T-Rex and crawled awkwardly over to him. The smell of freshly cleaned leather reached her nostrils as she arrived at his feet. She bent and brushed her lips over the supple leather of each boot, then waited as commanded for further instruction.

"I'm going to ask you a question and the only thing I care about is honesty. There is no correct or incorrect answer." He paused for a moment as if letting her prepare herself for his next words. "Are you wet right now?"

Dripping. "Yes, Sir," she said so softly she wasn't sure he could hear her.

"Are you ashamed of that?"

Slow tears slid down her cheeks at the soft words. "Yes, Sir."

"Don't be. That's just how you react to this kind of stimuli. Stop worrying about what it says about you or how weird you are, or anything else. Just be. Not a single person here is going to judge you for it. We are molding you into what we want you to be. Obeying us pleases us. Forget everything from before. It won't serve you here."

She'd had her hands in her lap, staring at his boots, listening as the words fell over her. One half of her wanted to rebel, scream, fight, because she hadn't said any of this was okay. The other half felt peace for maybe the first time ever, no longer drifting in some listless sea unsure of her purpose and unable to find one.

Vivian wanted to grab the peace and never let go, but she was afraid if she did, she would lose herself completely. She was scared to look in the mirror and see a shell instead of a person, a set of conditioned responses instead of a personality. She wanted to pour all of this out on Gabe, in hopes that he would understand or comfort her, but she couldn't.

Not only because she might be punished for speaking out of turn, but because entrusting him with her deepest feelings and fears only moved her in the direction of that fear. The only self-protection left was keeping her feelings and thoughts to herself, even as she knew they would be changed by these powerful men holding her prisoner.

She flinched when she felt his hand unexpectedly petting her hair.

"There's a lot going on in there, isn't there?" he said.

"Yes, Sir."

"Everybody feels these things in the beginning. You'll be just fine. I promise."

Promises from a criminal—from one of a gang of criminals—weren't as reassuring as promises from someone sane and upstanding would have been. But criminals and victims were all she was surrounded with anymore.

She felt him tugging gently at her and pulling her to her feet. He took a key from his pocket and unlocked the cuff. She stared at his big hands as they encircled her wrists. To an untrained eye, her gaze averted from his might have been seen as submission, but it was embarrassment, shame. She knew Gabe must know it. He'd seen this too many times. But he didn't taunt her; he just inspected her wrist.

"You're a little chafed. You must toss and turn like a madwoman in your sleep."

She didn't say anything.

"I'll have someone come by to switch this out for a cuff made out of something softer with a lining, so it won't hurt you."

She looked up, shocked. "Thank you." She hadn't expected the small kindness or the concern.

He held her gaze trapped in his. "I told you, we aren't complete monsters here. We are selling healthy, well-trained slaves to men who can afford the very best. We

are not selling broken dolls no one wants to play with."
He took her hand and led her to the bathroom.

She felt herself once again falling under this bizarre
seduction. The way she'd let herself go with Anton on
the massage table until forced orgasms seemed like an
idea she'd thought up.

And now, she felt herself being seduced once again,
first by the gentle lovemaking of Annette the night
before, and now by Gabe. The house must be run like a
well-oiled machine. Everything so calculated. How many
different trainers would she have? And would each of
them possess this much self-control?

Even when Anton was angry, he'd used enough
restraint to keep himself from harming her. He'd seemed
upset to be causing her distress, which felt at odds with
the situation. If one didn't want to cause women
distress, a great first step would be not running a training camp for sex slaves out of your mansion.

Vivian wondered if Anton could truly care for
Annette. Had they forged a bond stronger than the kind
of puppies and kittens love she'd had beaten into her
brain by fairy tales and Disney movies? Could she have
the same? Did she want the same?

She watched as Gabe stripped off his clothes and
started the water in the shower. His tan highlighted
muscles he'd obviously worked hard for. She wanted so
badly to ask why he, Lindsay, Anton . . . why any of
them would take a job like this or start a business like
this. They could have anyone they wanted.

Vivian took his offered hand and let him guide her
into the shower, let him position her, and place her
hands flat against the tile. She listened to the click of
the shower gel lid popping open and then the squirt as
he squeezed some onto a loofah.

He lathered her body while his back took the hot, pounding of the spray, then he put the loofah aside and used his hands to massage each inch of her, kneading her flesh and turning bathing into foreplay. His hands played over her breasts, tweaking her nipples, then plunged between her legs and the cleft between her cheeks. He was more gentle as his hands moved over the bruises Anton had given her.

He bent next to her ear, his voice low. "Last night, we had a contest. Whoever could jerk themselves off the fastest while watching you and Annette going at it, would win the right to bathe you every morning until you're sold."

She felt her knees start to give out, not wanting to support her weight anymore, but a strong arm gripped her around the waist and held her steady. She couldn't stop the desperate little sound that left her mouth.

"I feel much the same way, lover," he growled in her ear. "And of course, that was only one half of the prize. The other half, is that I get to have you bathe me."

His fingers slipped between her legs, stroking her. "If you get close, you ask me to come. If you come without my permission, you will be punished."

She bit her lip and nodded. He continued the teasing torment but didn't let her get close enough; he wanted her on the edge, and she knew it. He wanted her so horny she'd do whatever he asked, so lost in the haze of unrestrained arousal, she wouldn't have time to analyze it and feel ashamed or traumatized.

He moved her under the water to rinse her, then placed the loofah in her hands. "Lavender is a bit girlie. I'll bring my own tomorrow. Today, I don't mind smelling like my newest toy."

Being called his toy should have pissed her off. It should have hurt her. But all it did was start that mindless hum between her legs. The feeling was so strong she started to rub herself against his thigh.

"Don't be naughty, Vivian. Touch me. Wash me."

He switched places so she was under the water and positioned his hands on the wall, spreading his legs so she had full access.

She lathered him using the loofah as he had done, then switched to massaging. He let out a hiss of air when her hands were on him. Vivian felt a surge of feminine pride that she affected him so strongly with a simple touch.

Her hands slid over his broad chest, his back, his neck and shoulders, his legs. She rubbed and stroked everything but the one thing he wanted stroked. He let her play and tease at first, but then his voice came out hard.

"Your hands. On my cock. Now."

"Yes, Sir." As the words fell from her mouth, they sounded husky. Was she flirting with him? She was undeniably attracted, but if there was a rulebook out there with behavior tips for captivity, flirting with one of your captors was probably on the *don't do this* list.

But she couldn't help it. He was right. She wanted him. She wanted Anton. She wanted Lindsay. If that made her a slut, fuck it. If that made her a whore, who cared? It wasn't as if she were being given a choice in this charade to begin with. Clearly she'd been wired all wrong, but if that would protect her, why not embrace it?

A throat cleared. "Vivian?"

Had she really just gone off on a mental vacation and forgotten the impressive cock in her hand? "I'm sorry, Sir."

"I think you want to be punished," he said, a hint of teasing in his voice.

She didn't reply to that, mainly because she wasn't sure which answer would be the lie. And she didn't feel like exploring it when she had something much more interesting to explore.

He was thick and hot in her hand, and she could barely wrap her fingers around him as she started to jerk him off. His hips began bucking against her as she found a rhythm.

"Vivian, look at me. Look in my eyes."

*Please, no.* She wanted to hide. She'd become an expert at the art. *Don't make this more real. Not yet,* she silently pleaded, still staring at his cock bulging in her grip.

"I won't keep giving you warnings and second chances. Look in my eyes, and don't look away."

Vivian obeyed. His eyes were wild and lust-filled. She wasn't sure what hers held, but she didn't want him looking that far into her soul to see the jumble of conflicted emotions.

Their gaze was locked for what felt like hours, but was probably only a couple of minutes. His eyes said, *Accept this.*

She wanted to.

For a moment the two of them were suspended in time, not even the hot pelting of the shower existed. Then he ripped her hand off his cock and spun her around, bending her at the waist so her hands were flat on the tub beside her feet.

With one sharp thrust, he was inside her. Vivian's walls contracted around him. He was at just the right angle, hitting her g-spot over and over until she couldn't think or remember her name. Right before he came, she did, mumbling incoherently. When he'd finished, she froze, her breathing heavy, her anxiety rising. Waiting for it.

"I believe I told you not to come without permission, did I not?"

She trembled, barely holding herself up. He was still inside her, his hands on her hips.

"Yes, Sir." The waterworks started again.

"Crocodile tears won't garner you pity. You receive mercy in this house through obedience."

She tried to stop crying, but it was one thing to take punishment on unmarred flesh. On top of bruises was more than she could cope with.

He pulled out of her and shut off the shower, then scooped her up and carried her back to the bedroom. He held her in his arms, both of them still wet and dripping and let her cry on his shoulder.

She was whimpering and babbling, "Please, Sir. I didn't mean to. I'll be good. I still have bruises from before, please . . ."

"Did I say I was going to hit you there?"

"You said earlier you'd flog me." Her words were muffled into his shoulder, but he seemed to hear them, or at least get the gist of them.

"But I didn't say I'd flog your ass. You've got a lovely back I can use for a canvas, do you not?"

"Yes, Sir."

The door opened then. Vivian looked up to find a man she hadn't seen before, standing in the doorway with a silver bracelet in his hand. Vivian burrowed back into Gabe's neck.

"You've got this one crying already?" the man remarked, impressed.

Vivian heard the other man's footsteps moving closer and found herself cringing away, burrowing so hard against Gabe, she may as well have been clawing to get inside him.

"Not now, Brian. She needs more time. You start in on her before she's ready, and we'll break her too far. Anton won't be pleased."

Brian cursed. "But I like new toys."

"Did Anton even say you could play with this one? As far as I've been told, he wants only me and Lindsay touching her."

"That's not how he normally does things."

Vivian could feel Gabe's shrug against her skin. "Talk to Anton. Leave the bracelet with me."

Brian made an agitated sound and left. When he'd gone, Gabe pulled her away from his shoulder. "You will be punished for the shower incident, but I haven't decided what I'm going to do yet, so you're safe for now. All right?"

She nodded as he wiped her tears away with the pads of his thumbs.

"Give me your wrist."

He unlocked the plain, silver band and secured it around the offered wrist. "We'll lock the other chain around your other arm when you're to be confined to your room. This band will allow you to go outside to a certain point and around the mansion. There is an invisible fence. If you cross it, you'll be electrocuted.

"It will incapacitate you. We'll come get you, and the punishment will be worse than anything you can imagine. The mansion and grounds are equipped with security cameras, and if we see you fiddling with the bracelet trying to get it off, you'll face a similar punishment. Are we clear?"

"Yes, Sir. I can leave this room?"

He chuckled. "Well, I certainly wasn't going to serve you breakfast in bed. There are some gym clothes in one of those drawers." He pointed.

She looked away, not wanting him to know she'd already checked out everything in both rooms. If he noticed, he didn't comment.

"Put them on, and I'll take you to breakfast," he said.

Vivian unfolded herself from his lap and went to the drawer to get dressed. She knew he admired her bruised ass as she walked away from him. She could feel his eyes boring hot little holes through her skin. Tension and uncertainty hummed through her while she slipped the clothing on.

"Socks and shoes, too. A bit after breakfast you'll be sent to the gym to train. We can't sell flabby merchandise. And with the food here, it's easy to get flabby."

It was hard to assimilate everything. Gabe made her feel weirdly safe. He'd just protected her from being molested by Brian. And yet, he'd just done much the same thing himself.

If she was going to the gym after breakfast, it made some measure of sense that she'd be wearing gym-appropriate clothing. But she still found it hard to believe any of them would allow her the small measure of dignity normal attire afforded.

Gabe had retrieved his clothes from the bathroom. She glanced shyly at him as he pulled his shirt over his head.

"If you have any questions, I'll allow them right now. I know a lot of this must be confusing and weird for you."

Also criminal and evil, but she was trying to put that part on a shelf, since whining about her captivity wouldn't change the situation. She sifted through the questions that had bubbled to the surface since she'd been brought here, trying to find the most pertinent ones that hadn't already been answered. Even if he was allowing her a question and answer session, his patience wasn't infinite.

"What happens out there?" she pointed at the door. "How do I act?"

"Outside this room, you'll meet others like you. Try to get along. Some of them can be nasty, and more than one has been confined to her room for a week at a time for bad behavior. If you want my advice, interact as little as possible. They don't concern you anyway.

"Show respect to the men with proper address. They won't do anything too extreme to you out there. If they want to use you they'll bring you back to this room, or in some cases their room. You won't be expected to kneel or anything like that outside of these specific areas. When you are bought, your master might want something different. That'll be out of our hands."

"I thought only you and Lindsay were allowed to touch me?"

"For now. That may change. I'm not sure how Anton wants to handle you. Anything else?"

"No, Sir." It was a lie, but there was no way he could answer every thought flying through her head to her satisfaction.

# ELEVEN

In a mansion one might think the appropriate word would be *kitchen* or *dining room* or—considering the size of the space—*dining hall*. But it was more of a cafeteria. The room was large and noisy with a brunch buffet set up on one end.

Vivian was left to help herself with a parting warning from Gabe that if she overdid it past what she could work off in the gym, they'd restrict her eating. That threat held some level of menace considering the vast spread of food available. The mansion must have a few top chefs.

Hell, for all she knew, Gabe could double as a chef. Or that Brian guy. The more she explored, the more she felt like Alice down the rabbit hole. A stoned caterpillar wouldn't have shocked her at this point, and she would have gladly requested some of whatever he was smoking.

She looked at the many tables scattered about the room. There were around thirty girls eating and chatting. A few sat alone, looking uncomfortable. Maybe new like her? Or maybe women who had been burned by the nastiness of some of the others.

At the center table, Vivian easily spotted the queen bee. If there was such a thing as an alpha slave, she was it. Several girls crowded around the table hanging onto the queen's words. A moment later, they all laughed and looked over at Vivian, predatory interest in their eyes.

Vivian ignored them and loaded up her plate. When she turned, she was surprised to find the queen bee had gotten up from her table and now stood only a few feet away.

The woman had raven locks that fell to her waist. Her features were statuesque, and she appeared to be in her early twenties. "Wow. They're just bringing in anything off the street now, aren't they? What are you? Like forty?"

Vivian rolled her eyes. She wasn't sure what kind of catty sorority sluts movie this woman thought she was in, but Vivian was such a loner, social posturing had little effect.

She put on her best cheery, fake smile. "Let me guess. You were the prom queen, the homecoming queen, and the head cheerleader. Now all your power has been stripped, but somehow you lead everything here, too."

The queen bee's eyes narrowed. "You don't want me for an enemy," she hissed.

Vivian shrugged. "The way I see it, we're all in the same boat here. So go ahead and enjoy your last burst of feminist power while it lasts."

A few girls giggled in the background, and the queen's eyes widened. Vivian didn't see the fist coming, mainly because women like this one tended to scratch, smack, and pull hair. Not punch.

Vivian dropped her food to reflexively grab at her bleeding lip.

Within moments there was a flurry of activity as several men entered the room. Gabe came out of the crowd and stopped in front of the queen bee. His move to put Vivian behind him, keeping her out of range of a second punch, wasn't subtle.

"Sabrina," he said, harshly. "Did you forget we have security cameras?"

Vivian backed up a little so she could watch the queen. Sabrina's face held the same fake apology and confusion that many beautiful women could get away with. Hell, Vivian had played that trick and won a few times, herself. But Gabe seemed utterly unimpressed with the trembling lower lip routine.

Sabrina dropped to her knees and kissed his boots in a grand, sweeping show of submission. "I'm sorry, Sir."

Gabe backed out of her reach as she continued to abase herself. It was as if someone had pushed a mute button on the room as all chatter and eating stopped in light of the new unfolding drama.

Vivian could taste the copper tang of her own blood and felt a trickle running out from the corner of her mouth. She watched the scene with growing apprehension.

Gabe finally spoke again. "Sometimes I think Lindsay and Anton were wrong about you. You're far too resistant. Do you know why you've been here a year?"

"No, Sir," she said quietly. Vivian thought she could hear the barest tinge of derision in the woman's voice.

"Nobody wants you. We can't *give* you away. Potential buyers take one look at your behavior, and they don't want to shell out money for it. The few who have, through some sick need to break you, have all been turned away. You should live on your knees at Anton's feet, thanking him for the monsters he's saved you from. I honestly don't know why he bothers."

Vivian saw the subtle shift in Sabrina's body, the little cringe.

"We try to do what's necessary so our girls will have an actual personality when they leave this place. We thought socializing you with each other would be a good idea. But we're rethinking that. At least for you. In order to make back our investment, you'll have to be broken almost completely. You will spend the rest of your time until you're sold in your room. You will not see anyone except for the men you service."

"NO! Please, Sir. I'm sorry. I'm sorry. I'll be good. I won't cause anymore trouble." Sabrina shot Vivian a look so cold that she flinched. The other woman's gaze promised retribution. Even if it was an empty threat, it was still scary. Sabrina had obviously gleaned a sense of power from the way she lorded it over the other women.

Brian and another man came forward and pulled her off her knees.

She kicked out and struggled. "You can't do this to me!"

"We should have done it in the beginning. We've been far too lenient with you, and it ends now. You've always kept your behavior just this side of unacceptable, but assaulting another girl will not be tolerated."

"Please, Sir . . . please, I'll do whatever you want. I'll blow you, right here, right now."

Gabe chuckled. "If I wanted you to blow me here, you'd do it anyway. You belong to us. You have no chips to bargain with."

She continued to wrestle uselessly against the grips of the men who held her. Finally she gave up the fight, the fire going out of her eyes. Gabe nodded once, and they dragged her off.

He turned toward Vivian, his anger still palpable, and she took an involuntary step back.

"Come here," he said softly.

She moved toward him, afraid she'd be in trouble for baiting the other girl. She didn't throw out empty apologies because the truth was, she wasn't sorry. She wasn't sure the woman deserved total isolation, but she had deserved what Vivian had said. And it was Sabrina who had chosen to escalate the situation beyond mere cattiness.

"We need to clean you up and get some ice on this. Did you even get to eat anything?"

"No, Sir." She looked at the scattered food and bent to clean up the mess.

"Leave it, and come with me."

The other girls went back to their breakfast and conversation as Gabe led her away. He'd been so cold to Sabrina that Vivian was suddenly afraid of having that hardness turned on her.

In the midst of her captivity, he'd shown her kindness, and she didn't want to admit how afraid she was of that kindness ending. They went down a couple of hallways. At the end of the second was a spacious bathroom with a Jacuzzi that seemed more for socializing or orgies than bathing. He gestured for her to sit on the edge of the tub while he sorted through drawers and cabinets.

When he returned, he knelt beside her, using a soft, wet cloth to wipe the blood from her chin and lip. He held her face to the light. "She clocked you a good one."

Vivian caught his smirk. "Are you upset with me?"

"No. I should thank you. I've told Anton forever she was going to do something like this. I was waiting for the opportunity to get her away from the rest of the girls. You might have a bruise by tomorrow. It doesn't look too bad, though."

Annette came through the door then and handed an ice pack to Vivian.

"Tell Anton I said I told you so," Gabe said.

Annette shook her head quickly. "Please don't make me say that. He's pissed enough."

He laughed. "All right. I'll do my own gloating."

Annette nodded, relieved, and took that as her cue to leave.

"I want you to keep the ice on your lip for a few minutes, then we'll get you fed," he said, combing her hair with his fingers.

"Can I stay in my room?"

"To eat?"

"For good. Until I'm sold."

He arched a brow. "Sabrina is the biggest trouble maker, and she's no longer a concern."

"What's the point of being around them? If I make a friend, I'll lose her forever. If I make an enemy, it's just more drama."

He seemed to consider her request. "You'd still have to go to the gym."

She waited, afraid to say the wrong thing when he looked so close to relenting.

"There's a library here, and many rooms you'd be free to explore when no one's using you." She knew he saw her cringe at that, but he didn't acknowledge her discomfort. "There's even a pool outside. You could think of this place as a resort."

She would never think of this place as a resort.

He was silent for a moment, then lifted the ice pack from her face to look at the swelling. He pressed it back against the corner of her lip and sat back, observing her.

"Tell me why. This can't just be about being anti-social. You could avoid the other girls by ignoring them and going about your business. Others here do."

Vivian stared at some point on the tiled floor on the other end of the room. She took a long time to answer, but Gabe didn't push. He seemed willing to wait forever for her to find a coherent order for the jumbled thoughts in her brain. Finally, she took a deep breath.

"It's too hard to live both ways. Feeling like property and also feeling like a guest. You've made my situation clear. If I'm property, I can't stand to feel like I have more freedom than I really have."

"You have the freedom we grant you. Once you're sold and have bonded fully to your new master, it's unlikely you'll be locked in a cage all the time. It isn't practical. You need to be able to handle the illusion of freedom. If we keep you locked in a room all day, how can you learn that?"

"You're leaving Sabrina locked in a room," she countered, hoping it didn't sound petulant.

"I'm sorry, Vivian. We aren't going to cater to your every whim. Go get your breakfast before the kitchen closes."

"Yes, Sir."

She started toward the door, but Gabe grabbed her hand and pulled her back to him. His lips caressed the corner of her mouth, and he whispered in her ear, "Don't let yourself become like Sabrina because you're afraid of this process. Your world is over. You're in ours now."

His hand slipped down to fondle her ass, and she dropped her head on his shoulder. Then his fingers moved underneath her gym shorts to stroke at the already moistening skin. It took little for Gabe to turn her on. She'd felt the chemistry between them the moment he'd first touched her.

He pulled away and gave her a little swat on the ass.

"Go."

Vivian wobbled, disoriented, then watched as he sucked the finger that had been inside her panties. She left while she still had the ability to walk.

# TWELVE

The cafeteria was empty when Vivian returned. She filled another plate, poured a glass of orange juice, then went to sit in a chair at one of the deserted tables.

She was midway through breakfast when she suddenly felt watched and looked up. Lindsay stood in the doorway.

She'd long given up thinking of him as Dr. Smith. Even if he was really a therapist, she couldn't see him that way anymore, and was grateful she was expected to call him Sir. It felt emotionally safer.

He stalked her, his movements sleek and lithe. The lines of his suit flowed off his frame like water, the same style he'd worn the day she'd met him in the office with all the orchids. Valentino.

He pulled a chair up behind her and sat with his legs wrapping around hers. She tensed at the intimate gesture.

"Eat, Vivian," he whispered in her ear.

She took another bite of pancakes as he spread her limbs apart.

"Keep your legs nice and wide for me."

"Someone might come in."

"If they do, I'll tell them to leave."

He gripped the front of her throat possessively, pulling her back against him. The grip wasn't tight enough that she couldn't eat. He was just sending her a message.

Vivian's hand shook as she put the glass of juice to her mouth. She winced when the acidic beverage touched her lip.

"Do you need water, instead?"

"Yes, Sir."

She heard the chair scrape out and experienced a momentary relief as he left and gave her space. The feeling was cut short a few minutes later when he placed a glass of cold water in front of her, then returned to his former position.

He used one hand to lightly stroke the front of her throat, while the other moved down to her shorts.

She tried to focus on her meal, but she couldn't taste any of the food. Her world had been narrowed to what was going on between her legs as Lindsay fingered her. That, and watching the door, paranoid someone would walk in.

She managed to get through her breakfast, hovering on the edge of orgasm, holding back the moans that were relentless in their quest to bubble to the surface. When she'd eaten the last bit of fruit off her plate, Lindsay's lips grazed the side of her ear.

"I told you you would lose all your inhibitions."

"Fuck you."

The doctor had always rubbed her the wrong way. *With the exception of right now,* her increasingly perverted brain supplied. His fingers hadn't gone underneath her panties. Instead, they'd played softly over the cotton material, driving her even crazier than skin on skin contact would have.

He laughed at her helpless squirming as she struggled to escape his touch. His fingers pressed harder, causing her to respond more than she wanted to.

"It's always a challenge," he said, "to know how much of a slave's fire to extinguish, and how much to let burn for the enjoyment of her future master."

She bucked against him, struggling to free herself but only succeeding in causing his fingers to rub against her clit faster. She came without warning, shuddering helplessly in his arms. When her orgasm had run its course, she sagged against him, panting.

"That's the orgasm you wanted in the coat room, isn't it?"

"Yes, Sir." Her cheeks were burning so much she knew they must be bright red, and anyone who might pass by the open doorway would see how embarrassed he'd made her. The thought of someone else seeing her so uncomfortable upset her more than them seeing her have an orgasm or give one to someone else.

Lindsay helped her to her feet. She didn't say a word as he ushered her down the hallway and back to her room. When they got there, Brian was sitting at the foot of the bed, his cock jutting out of the top of his unbuttoned pants.

The doctor nudged her into the room. "Crawl to him." His voice was so hard and guttural it made her jump.

"But . . . Gabe said . . . "

"I don't care what he said. Gabe isn't here right now."

She didn't know why Brian unnerved her so much. Maybe it was the way others acted around him, as if he were someone especially to be feared. She let out a piercing scream, hoping Gabe would hear.

Lindsay's hand clamped around her mouth. "I guess we'll have to gag you."

Brian spoke up from the bed. "She'll be useless to me, gagged." He pulled a little remote from his pocket and pressed a button.

Vivian jerked and spasmed in Lindsay's arms, her eyes widening as she looked at the dark-haired man on the bed. He nodded at the metal cuff around her wrist. The one that prevented her from leaving the grounds.

"That was a low-level shock. Call for help again, and you'll get more."

Vivian nodded quickly. She dropped to the floor and crawled to him, a knot forming in her stomach. When she reached his feet, she waited, her eyes downcast.

"I was just with a very dirty slut who humped my boot until she came shouting my name. I'll whip her for not using proper address later. I need you to clean them for me."

Her eyes jerked up to meet his. A slow smile spread across his face as he nodded. "Yes, exactly in the way you think."

When she hesitated, he ran a finger over the remote control. "Vivian, darling, I can give you much harder shocks. What you got was mild."

The threat snapped her out of indecision. She bent and trailed her tongue over the leather, tasting the other woman's juices. She felt Lindsay move behind her and pull down her shorts. A moment later a thin, lubed dildo was being worked slowly inside her ass.

"Relax," he said as he guided the toy gently in and out of her. She did, and was shocked to find the sensation somewhat pleasurable. If it had just been her and Lindsay in the room, despite her general distaste for him, she could have coped. But Brian was in front of her calling her a dirty boot-licking slut, asking her to tell him how much she enjoyed shining his boots for him.

He'd started moving, and she could tell by the angle of his body and the rhythmic sound of the mattress, that he was jerking off over her. He came a few moments later as the door slammed against the wall.

She turned to see Gabe standing in the doorway, looking so livid she wanted to crawl under the bed for fear it might be directed at her. But his gaze was leveled on Brian.

"I thought I made it clear you were not to touch her," he said, his voice so enraged it shook.

Lindsay had removed the toy from her ass, and she crawled away from both of them to Gabe, until she was leaning against his leg. His hand moved to pet the top of her head.

"Fuck, Gabe. What's so special about this one?" Brian groused.

"She was brought here too soon. If you dumb asses push her too hard before she's ready, she won't be fit to sell, and Anton will have all of our heads. Now get out."

Vivian cringed as Brian stood and zipped himself back up.

"What the fuck ever."

Lindsay followed, but Gabe stopped him with a hand on his shoulder. "You knew Brian wasn't allowed near her."

"I thought it would be okay if I was here. He wasn't as extreme as he normally is."

"That's not the point, and you know it."

Lindsay shrugged and left the two of them alone.

Strong arms reached under Vivian's elbows and pulled her up. She was too numb to think as Gabe carried her to the bathroom. He sat her on the closed seat, then shucked his clothes and turned on the shower.

"Get undressed and we'll get you cleaned up." His voice was a gentle purr that Vivian wanted to wrap around herself.

She peeled the T-shirt and shorts from her body, along with her panties, still wet from her orgasm during breakfast. She took his offered hand and climbed into the shower. He was silent as he washed Brian's spendings from her hair. Then he soaped the rest of her, as if instinctively knowing she'd want to wipe the whole experience off her. After she was clean, he turned off the shower and plugged the tub to run hot water.

When the it was deep enough, he sat and pulled her down into his arms, resting her head on his shoulder. She cried softly as he stroked her hair.

"You'll be okay," he said.

But his reassurance only made her cry harder. "Please take me out of here. I'll be yours. I'll do whatever you want. Please."

"I have nowhere to take you. I live here. I promise he won't be allowed near you again."

Brian had been as physically appealing as the rest of them, but he'd made her feel so dirty just by looking at her. She wasn't sure why she would so readily submit to Gabe when Brian turned her stomach. But she felt something human in those kind, green eyes that made it feel okay.

What if Anton sold her to someone soulless like Brian? She could see herself belonging to a man like Gabe or Anton. Hell, even Lindsay's type, she could in time grow to feel submissive feelings toward.

Gabe kissed her forehead. "Tell me what's going on in there."

Her voice was barely above a whisper when she spoke. "What if Anton sells me to someone like Brian?"

"He won't. He screens very carefully."

"Well, he hired him. Does he not screen carefully for that?"

She felt Gabe's body tense under hers and knew she'd pushed too far.

"Careful, Vivian. You already have a punishment coming from earlier this morning."

"I'm sorry, Sir."

The tension left his muscles, and he went back to petting her hair and back.

"Brian has his uses. Anton knows what he's doing. Don't worry."

Even the idea in abstract form of someone owning her, paying hundreds of thousands of dollars for the privilege, should have sent her into screaming fits. But instead it settled her somehow and took away the restless feeling she'd had for so many years it had sat as a background hum.

Since things had started with Anton, the hum had grown softer. Then when she came to the mansion, it disappeared altogether, leaving a blissful silence in its place.

"I don't understand what's happening to me," she said, her cheek resting against his pec.

"I know you don't."

"I don't feel like my reactions are normal. The most normal I've reacted was with Brian." Maybe Brian wasn't all bad if he could make her feel like a normal person having the normal response to what was happening.

"I don't want you to talk about yourself like you're abnormal. You have certain needs, and you aren't the only one. If you were, you'd be the only slave being trained in this house. Others have certain needs to own just like you need to be owned. We're in the business of matching those needs up. We're not just training you. We're watching you, seeing how you react to various stimuli so we can match you with the right master."

He made it sound like an online dating service. In her head she could see a list of sexual proclivities . . . likes kneeling, doesn't like kneeling, likes being called a slut, doesn't like being called a slut . . . She wondered if someone sat in a sterile office with a clipboard noting all this stuff down, and if she'd end up with a master like Gabe.

"Let's get you out of here before you turn into a prune. Pruny slaves are harder to sell."

She shouldn't have laughed; she shouldn't have wanted to. But in a weird way, Gabe made everything feel safe, and she wished again that he had someplace he could take her and that he wanted to.

He helped her out of the tub and dressed her in another pair of shorts and a t-shirt.

"Am I going to the gym?"

"You're going to talk to Dr. Smith."

She was about to argue, but the look in Gabe's eyes told her he was finished coddling her, and if she pushed any further she'd have another punishment coming.

Ten minutes later, Gabe had taken her down four different hallways and into an office. The office was a larger replica of the first one she'd met the doctor in. She stared at the orchids for a long time.

"Sit down," he said when Gabe had left them. She tensed now that the man she was starting to class as her protector had left her with someone she most definitely didn't feel safe with.

She sat.

He clasped his hands together and leaned forward over the desk. "Ms. Delaney, I apologize."

She cringed at hearing Michael's last name. She'd been trying to erase him from her mind. Trying to erase thoughts of him worrying, not being able to find her, of never seeing him again. That chapter had to be closed. For her own sanity.

"Ms. Delaney?"

She looked at Lindsay, not sure she could keep the disgust off her face.

"I didn't follow protocol. Even if Brian wasn't going to do anything too extreme, they don't want you fucking everything here. I should have respected that. I betrayed your trust."

Her mouth gaped. "You betrayed my trust the moment you sent me to Dome. What's a little boot licking and sticky hair added to that?"

He smiled. "I'm glad it didn't put your fire out."

She rolled her eyes and crossed her arms over her chest.

Lindsay took out a notepad and propped it on his knee, a pen poised over the paper. "One of my jobs here is to assess your psychological condition and how you're responding to training. I want you to talk to me about Brian and how that made you feel. Was it him specifically, or what he did or . . . "

Vivian just stared at him. "I can't talk to you about that."

"Why not?"

"Gee, let me think. You helped orchestrate my capture. You're one of my captors. Yeah, I'll just give you more weapons to use against me. Why don't I make a list of everything I'm afraid of while I'm at it. That way you have all the torture options in one place."

An exasperated look came over his face. "Let me put it to you this way. You will talk about this or you'll be punished, then you'll talk about it. And if I have to, I will hook you up to a polygraph machine. I can say I won't use this knowledge against you, but you won't believe me. And it doesn't really matter what you believe. You have no options here except to obey. Now tell me about Brian."

She looked at the orchids again. He was right, of course. But Anton's earlier exclamation about her intelligence had been rattling through her head since he'd said it.

"I don't know. It's too many different people. I just . . . I can't handle that many different people fucking me." He started scribbling down notes as she talked. "There's something very cold about him. On the coldness scale it's him, you, Anton, then Gabe. I can barely deal with you."

He smiled, still scribbling. "Noted. Is that all?"

Vivian shrugged, pulling at a stray thread on the gym shorts.

"What else?"

"I don't know. Maybe what he did, but maybe not."

"If it had been Gabe it wouldn't have upset you, would it?"

Her eyes shot to his, her face flaming. The last thing she needed was for them to think she had some kind of schoolgirl crush on one of them. Before she could answer, he spoke again.

"It wasn't lost on me how you reacted to him when he entered the room." Lindsay sat the notepad on the desk and propped his feet next to it. "Here is how we operate. We only hire attractive men because we want to make training easier. It also subtracts a variable so we can get a better read on your reactions to things. It's easier to get you to submit to beauty. And the easier it is for us, the quicker we can sell you and the more money we make."

"What good does that do me if you sell me to someone ugly?"

He chuckled. "You'd be surprised how rarely truly rich people are ugly. A lot can be done with money, and few people with that much of it go about looking like troglodytes. Some of the men here have different styles of domination. We let them all play with the girls to see how they react and respond. Then we can match appropriate masters with suitable slaves. I still think it was beneficial for you to have that experience with Brian. But I knew he wasn't supposed to be near you, and I was wrong to allow him to talk me into it."

Their discussion went on for an hour, the standard length of time if they'd been having a normal session out in the normal world somewhere. He quizzed her on her various feelings about what had happened so far, her submissive desires, her earliest sexual fantasies.

She found herself detailing slave and kidnap fantasies she'd never repeated to anyone, giving words and form to thoughts and feelings that had swirled in the darker, hidden regions of her mind, locked away for years. The feelings that had been awakened when she'd met Anton at Dome.

He forced her to admit her own complicity in where she was and the fact that the blackmail had been her permission to allow the fantasy to play out and pretend that she wasn't in some way responsible for it.

The openness with which she verbally expressed herself already showed in sharp contrast to the mousy, inhibited woman she'd been the first day she'd met the doctor. She could no longer work up shyness toward a man who had not only molested her in a coat room, but had recently been working a dildo in her ass. Talking about her sexual feelings was suddenly low on the scale of embarrassing and revealing with him.

By the time the session was over, he'd filled several pages. He glanced over the notes. "I'm very pleased with how well you're opening up. Come here." He crooked a finger and motioned for her as he placed the notebook back on the desk.

She rose from the chair and went to him as the lump formed in her throat again.

He sat, smirking up at her, no doubt reading the expressions play across her face.

"You're very transparent, Vivian," he said mildly.

"How so?"

She hated that he knew or felt he knew of some secret room in her psyche even she didn't possess the key to. Since she'd arrived at the mansion, she felt nothing belonged to her anymore, not even her own thoughts.

Two sides of her existed at war. One side felt peace, the other railed and fought, clawing to get out and free herself from the web she'd been snared in. The web she'd kept walking into, sure she could untangle herself, until it had gotten too sticky, and she was trapped by her own stupidity and perhaps desperation.

He shrugged. "Ask nicely, and I might tell you." He snapped a finger and pointed at the floor like she was some pet trying to climb up on the furniture.

The clawing, fighting side reared its ugly head as she glared at him. And before she could stop the words, they'd barreled right out of her mouth. "I'm not your dog."

He chuckled. "You're whatever I want you to be. Be wise, Vivian. I have quite a fondness for anal play. I'm sure we can find you a tail to crawl around in."

The other side of her responded as her stomach did a little aroused flip at the idea that seemed to both repulse and excite her at the same time.

"I don't want to have to punish you, and you don't want me to have to."

She sighed. She hated him, but he was right. She wanted to know what he'd been writing during their session. If he was willing to tell her, a little mild debasement wouldn't kill her. Not after everything else.

She dropped to her knees and tried to come up with something suitable to say that wouldn't sound like sarcasm. Maybe simple was best. "Please, Sir. Will you tell me?"

He shook his head. "Come, now Vivian, you can do better than that. I know you can. Somewhere in there is a deliciously naughty slut. You just have to let her out. What's the problem? Talk to me."

He'd pushed her head onto his thigh and was petting her hair.

"The problem is that I'm a prisoner being trained to service . . . "

"No more lies, Vivian. That's not the problem, and you know it. Don't take the easy out. What's the problem?"

She was crying now, her tears dampening his nice pants. "I don't know what you want from me when you ask me to do something so vague."

His fingers were still tunneling through her hair. "Are you self-conscious?"

"Yes, Sir."

"I'm looking for active participation, acceptance that this is your life now. You need to let everything go but the part of you you've been locking away. You need to open the door and let it out. Stop thinking. Start feeling. That's why you were shut down when you came to me the first day."

"This is wrong," she said.

"So are a lot of things that happen in the world. Are you going to debate your rights with me now? You have the right to freedom and to pursue happiness, and . . . Tell me Vivian, were you happy in your old life?"

"No, Sir."

"Well, then nothing is lost. Is it?"

She jerked her head up and just stared at him. Everyone in this asylum was fucked in the head. She wanted to dig her way out of the rabbit hole and go back to where life was normal. Where right was right and wrong was wrong. Where everything had its place and a neat little compartment. Where nothing was gray or backwards or upside down.

He raised an eyebrow. "When you came into my office that first day, you were upset that you couldn't achieve orgasm."

"No. I was upset Michael was making me see a sex therapist, like the problem was mine."

"Wasn't it? Did he not make an effort to help you come?"

She'd put her head back on his lap, not wanting to look into his eyes or let him see more of what lay behind hers. She sighed. "He did."

"So then the problem was on your end, was it not?"

She shrugged against his thigh.

"Everything has a price, Vivian. Due to your particular mental landscape, your body will only respond with complete surrender. If you wanted to be a cold, frigid bitch, you wouldn't have kept going back to Anton. You wanted what he could make you feel. You want what I can make you feel. Don't you? There is no harm in admitting it now. You're already ours. The only thing left is for you to accept it."

She nodded.

"Words, Vivian. Give me words."

"Yes, Sir. I want what you can make me feel."

She felt his movement, then heard the shuffle of belt buckles and zippers as he freed his cock.

"Now, ask me again to share with you what I gleaned from our session today. Don't think. Just feel."

Vivian looked at the long, thick cock. The fighting side of her was screaming in her brain like a banshee on drugs. Vivian mentally dragged her through the corridors of her mind until she found a dark hole to throw her down. Then, satisfied with the silence in her head, she scooted up until her breasts were pressed against his thighs.

She placed open-mouthed kisses along his hardened length, then licked up the side and around the head. She glanced up, her eyes locking with his, letting him know which side of her was in the driver's seat now.

"Good girl. Work me like a good little cocksucking slave, and I'll tell you what you need to know."

She went to work, moaning around him, shoving down all the stupid commentary in her brain that wouldn't let her just feel anything without analyzing it to death first. She tasted the salty tang of his skin, felt the drops of pre-come as they slid down her throat. She felt the fullness of him in her mouth, and the power in making him come apart for her, as he tangled his fingers in her hair, his breath leaving him in heavy, erratic pants.

She felt the pain where Sabrina had hit her, but still she kept going, ignoring it in favor of the almost hypnotic sounds coming from the doctor's throat.

When he'd finished, she sat back on her heels and looked up. "Please Sir, will you tell me now?"

He chuckled and mussed her hair. "There's hope for you, yet."

She blushed, still uncomfortable that she lapped up sexual praise like a dog when she should be fighting. Especially Lindsay.

He tucked himself back into his pants and righted his clothing, then he guided her head to rest on his thigh again as stroked her back.

"All right. Brian is a bit different, yes. You haven't truly seen his level of cruelty in action, but you're right to sense it. Of Anton, Gabe, and myself, you see me as the worst, Anton as a slightly lesser evil, and Gabe as the least evil. But that has nothing to do with what we're doing to you here or our dominance style. You see me as the most evil because I set you on this path and delivered you to Anton. Gabe is least evil because he just happened to be here when you got here. But we all know what we're involved in. We all work together to make this happen. There are no white knights in this house."

Lindsay was right, of course. She was being ridiculous. She'd already developed an almost romantic crush on Gabe, seeing him as her protector or rescuer, but he was just as much her captor as anyone else.

She expected the doctor to demand verbal surrender, making her accept he was right. But he didn't. Instead he helped her to her feet. His finger moved to her lip and lingered there.

"Does it hurt?"

"Yes, Sir."

"Why didn't you say anything?"

She shrugged.

"Not after all this progress, Vivian. Tell me."

"I knew what you wanted, and you knew I'd been hurt. But you still wanted it."

"I might have let you off the hook until you healed if you'd asked."

"You would have been disappointed," she said.

He smiled. "And that matters to you, doesn't it?"

"Yes, Sir. I don't want it to matter. It's wrong that it matters."

He nodded. "Do you understand why Anton brought you here now? You belong to us, and soon you'll belong to one man who can give you what you need. Is that what you want?"

She looked into his eyes for a long time, the banshee screaming and trying to get out again. He must have seen it too.

"Forget your old life and that world. The moment you can truly shut that door, you'll be free to feel what you feel. You're safe here."

She nodded, finally. "Yes, Sir."

"Are you going to trust us to take care of you and place you with a good master?"

"Yes, Sir."

He nodded. "It's almost noon. Why don't you go down to the cafeteria and get a sandwich or something? Maybe sit by the pool and get some sun. You're a little too pale."

She left the room, not sure why she felt so floaty and calm, but tired of fighting it.

# THIRTEEN

Without Sabrina to rule the roost, most of the cattiness had ceased. A few bikini-clad women splashed in the pool while Vivian lounged beside a small table. Taking Gabe's diet restriction threats seriously, she'd gotten chicken salad on a croissant, a bowl of pineapples, and a glass of water with lemon.

When she finished eating, she peeled her shorts and top off to reveal a pink and white polka-dotted bikini. Vivian reclined in the lounger and closed her eyes, absorbing the warmth of the sun. The doctor was right, she didn't get outdoors enough, which was ridiculous since she used to stay home all day. What would have been so hard about finding fifteen to twenty minutes to lay out and soak up the rays?

Calm was easy to come by with the sun warming her skin and a light lunch in her stomach. A shadow fell across her, and she lurched as fingers trailed down her thigh. She opened her eyes; a smile drifting across her face when she saw Gabe looking down at her.

He handed her a bottle of sunscreen. "I want you to get a little sun without lotion, then put this on before you burn. After that you can get your exercise in the pool if you promise to swim and not just splash around." He tossed a glance at the women playing in the pool.

"Yes, Sir."

"When you're finished, come back to your room. You've still got a punishment coming for climaxing without permission."

Her cheeks flushed as she looked around to make sure no one else had heard him, but everyone seemed engaged in their own activities. Then the embarrassment died away, and a lump formed in her throat as she started worrying about punishment and what it might entail.

Before she had a chance to respond, he slid his sunglasses over his eyes and went back into the mansion.

*Vivian swam like a mad* woman as if swimming laps in the pool could help her escape whatever Gabe had planned. Her faith in him being the *good one* was dwindling at the same pace as her energy. When she could go no more, she dragged herself out of the water. Her body ached as she trudged to her room, questioning the wisdom of causing herself so much pain when she no doubt would get more.

Gabe looked up when she stumbled in. He frowned. "Did you think I'd take pity and choose not to punish you if you wore yourself out?"

"No, Sir."

"Come here."

It was a relief to crawl across the floor, to not have to hold herself up after the abuse she'd heaped on her body in the pool. When she reached him, she pressed her lips to his boots, then waited, every muscle exhausted further from anxiety.

"Good girl. I didn't expect you to remember."

She wasn't sure whether she should be offended by that. Was her emotional resistance to the training that strong, or did he find her stupid? Between him and Anton she was going to develop a complex about her brainpower.

He was quiet for several minutes, and Vivian waited, unwilling to break the silence and make him more upset with her. Finally, he spoke again.

"Come with me."

She took the offered hand as he helped her to her feet and guided her through the mansion and down a steep flight of stairs until they reached the dungeon Vivian had known Anton would have. It was smaller than she'd expected, which led her to believe there must be more than one, for people who wanted some measure of privacy for punishments or play.

Gabe led her to stand between two sturdy poles that came up out of the concrete. A metal ring jutted from the top and bottom of each one, with a short length of chain attached to it.

"Take off your clothes."

He went to a large trunk on one side of the room without a backward glance. It was obvious he didn't want a show. Gabe was all business, and clothing would only get in the way of his plans.

Vivian removed and folded the gym clothes, then untied the strings of the still-damp bikini. She shivered as the air hit and hardened her nipples. He returned first with a blindfold and covered her eyes, preventing her from seeing what else he was bringing from the chest.

She stood still as he took each wrist and fastened a cuff around it, then brought it up to the chains on the poles. He repeated the action with her ankles until she was stretched wide, whimpering from the pain pulling her muscles.

"Next time perhaps you'll think twice about pushing so hard in the pool right before punishment. What were you trying to accomplish?"

"I don't know, Sir." But she did know. It was just too stupid to put into words that she'd been running from him and the punishment that had now caught up to her. She'd sound like a head case.

The room was quiet. Tension curled around her, a tangible thing, as she waited for whatever was about to strike her. Instead of pain, she felt Gabe's lips kissing a trail over her neck and shoulders.

"When you get close to orgasm, tell me. If you come again without permission you'll be punished in front of everyone in this house, including Sabrina. And it won't be pretty. Do you understand me?"

"Yes, Sir."

"What's about to happen is mild because this is all still new to you. Remember that after it's over."

Then he set to work on her, his fingers skimming over her skin, dipping inside her, circling insistently around her already swollen clit. Her arms were killing her hanging in the chains, but it still only took minutes for him to manipulate her almost to the point of orgasm.

"I'm close," she whispered.

He immediately stopped, as she'd known he would, leaving her hips to buck helplessly against the air, her body begging for release.

Moments later several strips of leather struck her back. She'd remembered the things she'd seen in the chest in her bedroom and his earlier threat about flogging. He brought the flogger down over and over until what started out an almost pleasant sensation, turned into a painful sting as her back became more raw.

She whimpered and cried out, "Please, Sir."

"Please, Sir? You disobey a direct order from me right after I told you not to this morning, and all you've got is 'Please, Sir?' You little slut. Give me something creative and maybe I'll stop for a few minutes."

Tears were already streaming down her cheeks, dropping from her chin and onto the concrete. "This slut is very sorry."

He laughed. "Third person speech. Aren't you the little overachiever now? More." The flogger cracked against her back again, drawing out a scream.

"Please, Sir. Your dirty slut is sorry she was bad. She won't disobey again."

She heard the flogger as it fell to the ground, and then his mouth was kissing over the skin of her back, soothing away the pain he'd just caused. It was wrong but also right to feel the softness of his lips caressing welts left by his hand.

Gabe went back to teasing her, his fingers stroking over her labia but not touching her clit or venturing inside. She twisted and turned to try to get his hands to bump against the right spots. Vivian knew it was foolish. He wasn't going to let her come, so striving for contact that would stimulate her wasn't her best move.

But she couldn't help it. He pulled his hand away, leaving her whimpering. The glass toy he thrust inside her next was long and wide, with large ridges. He fucked her without mercy, knowing exactly how to angle the toy to torment her the most. His mouth was next to her ear when he growled, "Don't come. Warn me first."

She nodded, biting her lip against the onslaught. He used his other hand to manipulate her clit. She was tempted to try to have a little orgasm. Maybe he wouldn't notice. But he would notice. And then she'd be punished in front of everyone, including the bitch who'd busted her lip.

That thought killed her libido enough so she could think straight again. "I'm close," she said.

He stopped.

"Tell me little slut, does your cunt belong to you?"

"No, Sir."

The flogger cracked over her back, and she cried out.

"Who does it belong to, then?"

"The house," she gasped.

He stopped completely for a moment. No words. No flogging. Just an agonizing suspension of nothing and blackness. For one insane moment she thought she'd died, and the oblivion had taken her, but she still felt the fabric covering her eyes. Then a sharp laugh rang out, bouncing against the walls.

"I think you're a lot smarter than you let on, Vivian. I expected you to say it belonged to me. I thought we'd have to go through about five successive questions before you got the right answer." He caressed her back as he spoke. "Who does your body belong to, slut?"

"The house, Sir."

She flinched as the flogger came down on her again.

"And what are you?"

She thought back to the words Anton had said to her at Dome, the words that had gone straight to her pussy and had made her ache with the need to be stroked to soothe away the feeling they'd caused. She paraphrased them now.

"I'm a series of warm holes meant for the house's pleasure."

He kissed the shell of her ear, then whispered, "Very good girl. I envy the man who buys you, you know."

She flushed with pleasure at the praise, and no longer gave a shit what that said about her.

He alternated between pleasure and pain, taking her to the brink, where she had to fight and claw to keep from falling over the edge of the cliff, then into a deeper pain each time he went to work on her with the flogger. She wasn't sure if he was increasing the force he put behind the blows or if her skin had become so tender that everything hurt more. She felt as if she'd left her body, like she was floating in a different orbit than the one she normally existed in. The sensation both scared and excited her.

Vivian wasn't sure how much time had passed like this. It seemed like hours, days even. He stopped all at once, and suddenly, without every sensation being focused on her back or pussy, she could feel the pain in her arms again as she hung from the chains. And truly she was hanging. Without the strong chains holding her up, she would have collapsed to the ground long ago.

In testament to this, when Gabe unlocked her wrists, she dropped to her knees, her cheek resting on the floor. Every part of her was exhausted, limp, achy. A part of her was more satisfied than she'd ever felt before, but another part was so consumed with the need for orgasm that she couldn't stop the wracking sobs as they tore out of her.

Gabe didn't comment. He unlocked the cuffs around her ankles, and checked them and her wrists for damage.

"Wiggle your fingers and toes for me."

She did.

"Good girl. Now roll onto your back. I know you can't hold yourself up right now."

She rolled over, praying he would finally let her come. The cool concrete was a balm to her heated skin.

"Do you think you've learned your lesson?"

"Yes, Sir," she said. *Please please please let me come.*

Though she couldn't see him, she felt his strong presence as he stood over her. She imagined he must be looking down, his arms crossed over his chest as he admired the results of his work.

"I'm not sure. I want to be sure. Stay," he said.

As if she had the power to go anywhere. She had no idea how she'd manage to get out of the dungeon as it was. His boots thudded across the floor back to the big box of torture devices. She held her body rigid as he rifled through the contents of the chest, fearing what awful thing he might bring back with him.

Moments later he was rubbing a cream on her clit, the same one Anton had used at Dome. Her need climbed to an even higher peak than before. It took every ounce of willpower not to move her hands between her legs, even though she knew he was watching, and she'd just be punished again.

Then he was pulling something hard over her legs and locking it in place. Her pussy was covered now with something so unyielding, she couldn't have gotten off no matter what she did. She let out a little sob, half anguish that he wasn't finished torturing her and half relief it wouldn't require her to use self-control she was no longer physically capable of.

"I told you I didn't want to have to put a chastity belt on you, Vivian. But we do what we must. Your punishment will be over in the morning. If you have to go to the bathroom, let one of us know and we'll take you."

"Yes, Sir."

Even after everything he'd done to her, and maybe because of it, she wanted to snuggle up next to him. She wanted to kneel at his feet and lay her head on his lap as he pet her hair. The only thing she could feel, beyond the relentless awareness of her arousal, was her need to please him. To submit.

She felt a brief sense of dizziness as Gabe unexpectedly scooped her up and carried her to her room. He laid her on the bed, took off the blindfold, and brushed her hair back from her face. "Rest, lover. I'll wake you for dinner."

She nodded as her eyelids drooped, and despite the incessant, throbbing need, sleep claimed her.

*In her dream she was running down a long hallway with many doors. A dragon chased fast on her heels. If she could just get through one of the doors, she'd be safe. They were too small for the dragon. Even if he could tear down the wall to continue the chase, it would give her a head start. She could hide.*

*But every possible escape was locked to her. She finally ran out of hallway, with one final exit ahead. The basement door of her house. But Michael kept that door locked. She reached out anyway, desperate.*

*The doorknob clicked open in her hand. As she pushed it, she could see a light at the bottom of the stairs and a shadow moving below. Michael?*

*She gripped the rail of the stairway, but before she could get to safety, the dragon's claw wrapped around her ankle, dragging her back down the hall. She screamed for help, but the basement door slammed, shutting out her cries. Everything tilted and suddenly the door was above her. Her hands scrabbled for purchase as she struggled against the monster. But there was nothing to stop her descent. The floor was too perfect, too polished.*

*The dragon picked her up and tossed her down a hole, and she was in a free fall.*

*Vivian jerked awake from the* falling sensation, still screaming. She cowered away when she spotted Gabe, Anton, and Lindsay standing over her bed. Her conscious mind may have accepted her situation, even craved parts of it, but the banshee still struggled in her sleep, trying to shake Vivian up and make her fight harder, or at all.

But even after only a few seconds of consciousness away from the dream, she felt safe and warm. Even surrounded by the dragons. Maybe because she was surrounded by them. Everything had tilted.

"Are you all right, flower?" Anton. She'd missed him and his pet name that was somehow so dirty. Whether it was the innuendo he'd placed inside the word, or his wicked accent, she couldn't be sure. She'd miss him when she was sold. And Gabe. She wasn't sure about Lindsay yet.

"Do you need to use the bathroom?" Gabe asked.

"Yes, Sir."

He helped her out of the bed, and she winced.

"Jesus, Gabe. You hit her hard enough, didn't you? I'm surprised you didn't draw blood," Lindsay said when he could see her back.

She flushed, still embarrassed being naked in front of them.

"She'll heal. She had to be punished. I do it right the first time so the behaviors aren't repeated. You should try it. Would save you a lot of training grief."

Vivian glanced over at Lindsay to find him giving her a look she could read as if he'd dumped an entire conversation in her brain. It was as if he were saying, *I'm not as bad as Gabe. You calculated your hierarchy of evil wrong.*

But it didn't matter. She still felt affection for Gabe, and Lindsay still scared her. She knew it was irrational now that everybody's mask had been dropped to reveal who they were underneath. She just shrugged at the doctor, and he shook his head as if she were a lost cause.

Gabe took her to the bathroom and unlocked the chastity belt. She sighed when he leaned against the wall. Of course he wouldn't give her privacy.

"I'm sorry, I don't trust you won't try to touch yourself."

Between her nightmare and waking to the pain of her back, orgasms were the last thing on her mind. She wasn't about to try to rub one off in the bathroom. But she didn't bother trying to explain it to Gabe. She'd already peed in front of Anton, but she had to do a bit more than that, and she couldn't do it with an audience.

"Please Sir . . . I know you don't have to, but I really need privacy. I don't just have to pee, and I can't . . . with you standing there." She held her breath, praying he had the shred of mercy she believed him to have.

Finally, he poked his head out the door and called into the bedroom, "Lindsay, bring me some rope."

A minute later, Lindsay was in the bathroom, smirking down at her as he passed the rope to Gabe. Then thankfully, he left.

Gabe tied her wrists with such expert precision, she was sure he must have been a boy scout before he went evil. Then he tied the other end to the shower bar, causing her arms to go at an awkward angle. "This is the only way you get privacy. I'll be back in a few minutes."

The door shut quietly behind him.

He returned several minutes later to untie her so she could wipe and flush. "Don't linger," he said, as if she was going to try to masturbate her clit while she wiped.

She fought back an eye roll. Vivian was so not in the mood for sex, it was almost amusing how he thought she would be.

She expected him to put the chastity belt back on, but he ordered her into the shower instead. He stripped off his clothes and joined her. As his hands roved over her body, the soap working into a strong, fragrant lather, the libido she thought had died with the nightmare, came roaring to life again.

He didn't try to fuck her, and she suspected it was because he'd either fucked someone else while she was sleeping, or intended to once the chastity belt was locked in place again. She felt irrationally jealous even though he wasn't hers to possess. And even though their association would end once she'd been sold.

She shuddered at how casually she thought of herself as sold off to be some man's slave. Some man she didn't know. She wondered if she'd grow attached to him, if she'd love him, if he'd have any kind of feelings for her.

Gabe shut off the shower and wrapped her in a towel, guiding her out onto the tiled floor. He lingered over her clit, teasing. Vivian's eyes widened when he produced the tube of arousal cream. He couldn't be serious. But he was. He put a healthy amount on her and slipped the chastity belt over her thighs.

"Stay," he said.

Every time he said *stay,* she felt like a dog. She wondered if *roll over* or *fetch* would be next. But she stayed, standing in the warm, steam-filled room until he returned.

When he came back, Vivian's eyes widened.

"I decided to make your last bit of punishment more interesting."

He'd returned with another chastity belt. Only this one had smooth metal protrusions, one larger, meant to go inside her pussy, and one smaller, meant for her ass. She clenched involuntarily as she stared at it.

Gabe lubed both pieces of metal, then unlocked the belt she wore to trade it for the other. He carefully worked each of the phallic-shaped objects into their appropriate holes. She gripped the wall for support when he flicked his thumb over her clit, swollen and engorged from the arousal cream. He locked her up, then playfully swatted her thigh.

"Put some clothes on, and go eat your dinner. The day's almost over. Tomorrow will be better for you."

"Yes, Sir." She walked out of the room, close to passing out from the arousal and sense of fullness without completion.

# FOURTEEN

Vivian could barely taste her food as she chewed and swallowed. Her entire world was focused on the parts of her locked away behind the chastity belt. She couldn't stop squirming in her seat, but the belt was so fitted to her size that such movement didn't allow satisfaction.

She glanced surreptitiously around the cafeteria at the other girls, wondering if any of them suspected the punishment that had been visited on her. As she watched this woman or that shift in her seat, she wondered if they'd been given a similar punishment for some reason. Was the discomfort because they had cane welts across their ass, or was it because they had something shoved inside them and trapped there like Vivian did?

Everything under the belt strained and begged for release. She would have done anything, debased herself in any way, even in front of everyone, if it would mean she'd be permitted to come.

Gabe stood to one side of the room, his arms crossed over his chest. He seemed smug and pleased with himself, and yet she couldn't work up any hatred for him. She was already beginning to feel owned by these men, by the house.

Moments later, Lindsay approached Gabe. She watched, frozen, as the doctor whispered. He looked over at her a few times while delivering a long and private monologue, leaving no doubt she was the subject of his visit.

Gabe nodded once and handed the other man a key. Lindsay stared at her and smiled. She shuddered and went back to her food. The heated look the doctor had just given her was terrifying. And yet, her body responded. She tried to focus on her food, on the flavors exploding over her tongue, but it was even more useless than before she'd spotted the two men plotting.

As soon as she'd finished, Lindsay was in front of her, his hand outstretched. "Leave your plate, and come with me."

If he had the key did that mean her punishment was over? Or was it transmuting into something else? She expected to be led back to her room, or the dungeon, but instead they ascended a large, winding staircase. The one she'd seen in the entryway upon first arriving.

He kept her hand in his, leading her off like a lover instead of a slave. And she wondered if he really was more kind and merciful than Gabe, if she could trust him not to hurt her. They traveled down a hallway until they reached a door at the end. Instantly her mind flashed to the dream, and all at once the door to Lindsay's room created an irrational feeling of safety.

The anxiety that had swirled through her system since seeing the doctor during dinner, settled, leaving nothing in its wake but arousal. He pushed the door open and gestured for her to go inside.

The room was like nothing she'd ever seen.

"Horticulture is a hobby of mine. I like to watch and help things grow," he said, in response to the question she knew must have burned behind her eyes.

She tried to ignore the double entendre.

"You may look around if you wish."

So many plants. It reminded her of the *restaurant in the middle of a jungle* feeling she'd gotten at Dome. Orchids of every variety and size flourished in pots all over the room. There were exotic tropical flowers she wasn't as familiar with, with lush, full blooms. The floor had a dark green carpet, thick and plush, that made her feel as if her feet were sinking in soft grass.

An imposing king-sized canopy bed stood against one wall with a duvet in the same rich shade of green. Mosquito netting hung around the outside, enclosing the bed, as if they were outdoors and subject to a flying insect threat.

Three large bird cages stood spaced evenly about the room. One held a parrot, and the other two, several parakeets. The birds stared at her, chirping away, further heightening the room's strange and exotic feel.

Where the carpet ended, green plants and small trees in pots lined the walls in bunches. The floor beneath the plants was concrete with small drains. Vivian's brows drew together in confusion over this design choice.

"Look at the ceiling," he said.

Vivian looked up. Hundreds of tiny tubes protruded from the ceiling. Lindsay pressed a button on the wall, and she could hear the indoor rain as it pelted over the plants and swirled down the drains.

"This is incredible."

He moved behind her and peeled the clothes from her body. She melted against him as his hands moved to cup her breasts and stroke over her belly. One hand dipped to press possessively against her sex over the belt.

"Tell me who this belongs to right now," he growled.

"You, Sir."

His mouth was still close to her ear when he said, "Tomorrow I'm going to fuck your ass against that wall while the rain comes down on us. It'll be nice and warm. Would you like that?"

The idea of anal sex still scared the hell out of her, but he made it sound so soothing and decadent that the only thing she could do was nod and whimper, "Yes, Sir."

He turned off the water and guided her to a large, bathroom. Candles and plants lined the wide rim of a Jacuzzi tub. An impressive Georgia O'Keefe print hung on the wall opposite from the toilet. Ordinarily a print would seem odd in a mansion. But with the dampness of the air, Vivian understood Lindsay had to make the choice between his plants and original art. It was clear where his priorities lay.

He unlocked and removed the chastity belt. "Go to the bathroom, and then we'll sleep." He pointed at the ceiling. "I'll be watching to make sure you don't touch yourself, but I won't stand here in the room with you. Fair?"

A camera with a red, blinking light stared down at her.

"Yes, Sir."

He stroked her cheek then left her alone.

When she finished, he returned with yet another chastity belt and something else. When she saw the tube of arousal cream in his hand, she shook her head.

"Please, Sir, don't torture me anymore. I've learned my lesson, I swear." The cream Gabe had put on had just started to wear off.

"Don't fight me on this, Vivian. This is the last time. Tomorrow morning your punishment ends. I'll let you come when I fuck your ass."

He closed the toilet seat and motioned for her to sit.

"Be a good girl and spread yourself open for me."

Vivian sat and spread her legs apart, then pulled the flesh away from her clit. She could feel the heat and redness as the blush crept up her neck and into her cheeks. She felt open and exposed. Perhaps more exposed than she'd been with anyone else.

He sat on the ground in front of her to apply the cream, his eyes meeting hers. A soft expression came over his face. "You're so very sweet."

That only made her blush harder.

He rubbed the cream on and applied lube to the toys attached to the new chastity belt. She realized immediately why he'd gone to get another one. The attached toys were larger than what she'd been wearing the past several hours.

"That's too big. It won't fit."

"You better hope it does because it'll be my cock tomorrow."

He helped her step into the belt and eased the toys inside her.

"Stop holding your breath. Relax," he said.

She didn't know if she could *relax*, but she did manage to start breathing again, slowly in and out, letting out a sharp hiss at the pain. She whimpered plaintively as the lock clicked into place, feeling somehow claustrophobic from the double penetration she couldn't escape.

He kissed her on the mouth, his hand holding the back of her neck. "Such a sweet little whore. Tomorrow I'll make you come over and over for me. When I'm finished with you, you'll be begging for a chastity belt to get a break."

She just stared at him, sure her mouth hung open like a fish. But then he winked at her. The birds kicked up a racket when they reentered the bedroom. Lindsay covered their cages, causing them to fall quiet.

He gave her a cup of water and her pill. She took it without complaint.

"Get in." He pointed to the side of the bed he wanted her on. Vivian pulled back the mosquito netting and slipped underneath the covers. When he curled behind her, she looked over her shoulder to find his cock pressed against the belt. She squirmed, unable to forget the sensations below her waist. Afraid she'd never fall asleep like this.

"Be still," Lindsay said.

"I can't. It's too much."

"Lie on your stomach."

She obeyed, and he began to lightly rub her back, giving her something else to focus on. The soothing feeling went on forever, and just before she fell asleep she thought she might have already fallen a little bit in love with the doctor.

*Vivian woke to an insistent* mouth latched around her nipple and a hand pressed hard against the chastity belt. Lindsay's fingertips were stroking the insides of her thighs, sending flames of desire licking at her covered clit.

Her dreams had been peaceful. Sunshine, waterfalls, birds, and rolling meadows. Pretty puffy clouds floating overhead forming naughty little shapes in the sky. She moaned, as she came more fully awake under his ministrations.

"I'm going to let you use the bathroom, and we're going to shower first."

"I thought Gabe . . . "

His hand came down in a hard smack on her thigh. "I made arrangements with Gabe. When you are with me, I own your ass. Do you understand? There is no one else but me and my cock in this room."

Her eyes widened and she started to cry. "Yes, Sir."

Lindsay's lip pulled back in a snarl. "Don't give me tears. I didn't hurt you."

"I'm sorry, Sir." It wasn't the pain. It was the fact that one punishment was about to be over, and she'd already pissed off another one of them. She couldn't explain why, but she cared deeply when they were displeased with her.

He didn't bathe her like Gabe. It wasn't a seduction. Showering was a perfunctory experience, one that took time away from the other activities he'd rather be engaged in.

She felt almost violated from the way he washed her. Like a thing. When his soapy fingers moved into her asshole, the place he intended to use very soon, she cringed at the intrusion. It suddenly became clear this wasn't just about rushing through a shower so he could fuck her. He was still angry.

"I'm sorry. I didn't mean to upset you."

He grunted in response.

"Please . . . I want to make it up to you."

A beat of silence and then a sharp laugh that sent a chill skittering down her spine. "Oh. You will. Believe me."

That made her more afraid of him. Afraid enough that she felt compelled to diffuse the situation. "I wasn't expressing disappointment that Gabe wasn't going to shower with me this morning. I just thought that was the arrangement." Then her voice came out a little softer because she wasn't brave enough to say it anymore loudly. "I want you."

He turned her to face him and stared into her eyes for a few moments. "It doesn't matter if you want me or not. You're my fuck toy for the day, and you'll do as I say."

She might have started crying again if she hadn't seen his face. It betrayed him. His words were to maintain control of the situation. Perhaps it didn't matter if she wanted it or not, he'd have her anyway. But judging from the look in his eyes, he wanted her to want everything he did.

Lindsay shut off the water, passed her a towel, then dried himself with another. Without a word, he ushered her into the bedroom and pressed the button on the wall, making the rain come down. He removed the covers from the birdcages, and they started chirping and ruffling their feathers.

The African Gray started squawking, "Yes, Sir. Yes, Sir. Oh, God yes, harder."

Vivian didn't know whether to laugh or be mortified. Probably the only thing the parrot knew was dirty talk from the things he'd heard in this room.

"Shut up, Ralph. I'm not in the mood," Lindsay said.

"In the mood," Ralph repeated.

Lindsay snorted and covered the parrot's cage. The bird squawked and bitched and ruffled his feathers some more, then finally settled.

Vivian silently vowed she wouldn't call out anything during sex, no matter what the doctor did to her, for fear she or someone else would hear Ralph, the pervy African Gray, mimic it back.

"Are you scared, my lovely little whore?"

"Yes, Sir."

"Good. I like that. I want you to go stand under the rain, and step back from the wall enough so you can bend all the way forward. Use the wall for support."

She took a deep breath and did what he asked. The water was warm as he'd promised, like standing in the middle of a rainstorm during the hottest cloudy day of the summer.

She clenched involuntarily when his cock prodded at her ass. He smacked her, the sting sharper with her skin wet.

"Open."

He sighed when she remained frozen. Two lubed fingers massaged her opening. Her nerve endings flared to life, and she pressed against him. He took it as a cue to slide fingers inside.

She whimpered and relaxed as he slowly finger-fucked her.

"Listen to me, Vivian. My cock isn't much bigger than the toy you slept in. You took the toy just fine, and you'll take me just fine. I'm not going to hurt you. That's not the point of the exercise. I'm training you to like this, not be terrified of it for the rest of your life."

She nodded, relaxing a little more. A few moments later, he removed his fingers and eased himself into her. The pain was short-lived as she accommodated his size.

"Are you all right?"

That was all it took to release the flood gates. "Yes, Sir," she said through tears.

He didn't comment. Maybe he'd come to accept that nearly everything made her cry for one reason or another. He caressed her back as he used her, and she found herself moving, fucking herself on him.

"Such a dirty little anal slut."

She panted, pressing her hands harder against the wall as he rode her.

"Touch yourself. I want you to make yourself come. I want to feel you spasm and grip my cock like a good whore."

He could have fucked her with just his words and had her coming if he spoke like that for much longer. She moved her fingers between her legs and started rubbing.

A couple of minutes later he said, "Now. Vivian. Come now."

She wasn't sure if it was her fingers or his words, but she spiraled out of control at his command, sinking into an orgasm so strong she would have fallen if not for his hand wrapped around her waist, holding her steady.

"Keep going," he growled when she was about to stop. "Ride it out, as long as you can."

Her fingers obeyed him, dragging the orgasm past the point she thought she could stand it as he released inside her. Then he pulled her away from the wall and brought her to the floor with him. They laid together for awhile, neither speaking as their breathing came back to normal.

"Thank you, Sir," she said finally, still stupid-happy from her orgasm.

She could hear the smile in his voice. "Oh, you will be having many of those today."

He got up, leaving her sprawled on the carpet. Vivian couldn't bring herself to move, and he didn't ask her to. She watched as he got dressed in the designer clothes he always wore.

The distinguished gray at his temples and the little lines in the corners of his eyes only made him more attractive. He stared pointedly at her ass as he picked up his belt and looped it through the buckles. She knew he must be thinking about whipping her with it, and the thought sent a flutter of anticipation through her. He sat on the edge of the bed and put on socks and a pair of shiny dress shoes.

"Come here," he said.

She rolled over, her strength still not back, and forced herself to crawl the few feet to him.

He pointed at his shoes. "Thank me properly."

She bent and kissed the leather while he petted her hair. Then he wedged his foot in between her legs. Without thinking, she started to grind against him.

"Such a greedy little slut."

She stopped and looked up at him, unsure if she was in trouble for being so brazen.

He chuckled. "Go ahead, finish what you started, but know that I'm going to make you clean it up when you're done."

She felt her face grow hot, but rode him anyway until she came. Then she cleaned him as he'd asked, lapping up every drop of what had dripped from her body.

"I wish I could spend all day fucking you, but I have other work to attend to today."

Vivian was surprised to find that she wished he could spend all day fucking her, too. Her mind had given up on the *What is wrong with me?* mantra. What was the point? She was clearly fucked in the head. But she was tired of analyzing it, picking it apart, acting like she'd come up with a different answer if she just kept asking the question enough times. The answer was always going to be the same.

She got off on the things these men did to her. She missed Anton's hands on her body. Right now she missed Gabe, too. When Lindsay went off to busy himself with whatever he was doing for the day, she'd miss him as well. She'd miss his cock in her ass, the intense way he looked her, and his beautiful room that felt like an oasis from the scary new world she'd entered. Even though he had been the one to initiate her into it.

She was still naked on her knees, leaning her cheek against his leg as he absently petted her hair. Then he sighed and rose to his feet, jostling her in the process. She stayed next to the bed, waiting for an order.

A drawer opened and he shuffled through the contents. "I'm definitely not done with you today, but I have a nice toy to distract you while I'm off the property."

Vivian wondered if he was going to the other smaller office, the one where he'd entrapped her that first day. She wondered if he would fish today for more women to send to Anton and why she couldn't work up hatred for him even if that was true.

He returned with something that looked like panties, but she recognized it for what it was. It was a vibrator meant to be worn, pressed against the clit and surrounding flesh. Lindsay ordered her to put it on, and she quickly complied. He adjusted the straps so it fit snugly around her, then handed her clothes to put on.

"There is a remote. Actually there are multiple remotes. Ten of them, in fact, for this particular toy. I'll give one to Gabe and Anton, as well as the other men.

She wondered if Brian would get one. Her face must have telegraphed her fear because he nodded.

"Everyone. But Gabe, myself, and Anton are still the only ones allowed to play with you . . . really play. This is different. It's just someone pressing a button. Brian isn't allowed in your room. Don't worry."

She couldn't help worrying.

Lindsay sent her to breakfast with a swat on her ass and told her he'd see her later that afternoon after a warning that she wasn't to remove the toy at all, and if she did, one of the house cameras would catch her. He wanted her open and receptive to the vibrations whenever, wherever, and from whomever they were delivered.

At breakfast, she was self-conscious, trying to avoid the eyes of the trainers she didn't know, as well as Gabe's. She wasn't sure where Anton was, but she knew he'd been avoiding her to keep her from attaching to him too strongly. But it didn't matter. She'd attached to all three of her trainers already. Extra variety didn't matter.

If she'd been whored out to every man in the house, she still would have attached. It was who she was. She was standing in line with her tray to get food, when the vibrations started pounding against her clit. They began small, teasing, coaxing the little bud to swell with need.

Thankfully the toy was silent. She'd seen toys like it online, but this wasn't the more common brand. This was something expensive, probably custom designed for the house. As she put food on her tray, her eyes flitted about the room, trying to discover who was engineering her pleasure.

She was surprised to discover Anton standing in a corner nearby with a cup of coffee in one hand and his remote in the other. Aimed at her. She blushed bright red and looked to see if anyone had noticed, but no one seemed to.

Trying to ignore the increasing arousal, she went to sit at a table away from the few other girls.

A moment later she felt the vibrations increase, throbbing against her as she clutched at the table, working not to give her reaction away. She almost jumped when a hand landed on her shoulder.

"Come for me, flower. I've missed you."

She sat facing a window that went out onto a breeze-way covered in climbing yellow roses. Anton's wide frame at her back shielded her from view. Even so, she felt as if she were on display. The vibrator ratcheted up another notch, even though the last setting had been intense.

"Come. Now."

She wasn't sure if it was what he said, the fact that she'd missed that delicious accent, or the intensity of the stimulation going on below her waist, but the moment his words drifted to her ears, she gripped the table and came as quietly as she could.

When she was finished, he turned it off. "Good girl. Soon we'll find you a master. Would you like that?"

She nodded, a little moan escaping her throat as he ran his fingertips along the nape of her neck. He leaned next to her ear. "Before you go, I intend on one last fuck. I intend on using each of those lovely welcoming holes properly."

Then he placed his empty mug on the table and walked away.

The moment he'd left, Gabe approached. "Good morning, lover."

She flushed and looked at her plate, wondering if he'd found a position from which to observe her secret orgasm with Anton. "Good morning, Sir."

Vivian waited for the vibrations to start, assuming there would be a constant parade of men coming by to revel in the power they had to manipulate her body with the touch of a button. But the vibrations didn't come. Instead, he told her to go to the gym after breakfast, and gave her directions on how to find it. Then he left her to finish her meal.

She was disappointed he hadn't pressed the button. Gabe of all people. Was he still angry with her for coming without permission? Was he unwilling to give her any orgasm she didn't beg for or ask permission to have?

Those thoughts tumbled through her mind as she took her tray to the dishwasher and then made her way with trepidation to the gym. Would she be left to work out on her own? Would someone train her? Would it be Gabe, or someone else?

When she reached the gym, there were girls on treadmills and a few using weight equipment with trainers standing over them. Vivian stood awkwardly in the doorway not knowing what she was supposed to do now.

Then he was walking toward her. She had to stop the physical reaction to cringe or kneel, perhaps both, as Brian approached with a sadistic smile on his face.

"You're not supposed . . . "

The words hadn't gotten fully out of her mouth when he pulled a remote from his pocket—not the one to the vibrator. A sharp, electric zap hit her from the bracelet. Brian was the only one who used that particular power over her. Even though she knew they all must have it here.

In many ways it made her feel more helpless than being chained and whipped because there was no ritual or protocol that had to happen to set things up. No defined moment where the punishment would start and stop. With the remote for the band around her wrist, it could happen anywhere, at any time without warning. And Brian showed no hesitation in using it.

Even in the gym with other trainers and girls, she didn't feel safe with this man.

"I'm not supposed to come on you or fuck you. That doesn't mean I'm not allowed to train you or punish you in the gym." His voice came out a low snarl. He retrieved the other remote, the one that went with the toy and then his voice calmed to something approaching civilized human speech. "We're going to have an interesting session today."

Interesting was a word only a true sadist would use to describe their session. He pushed her harder than she'd ever been pushed. When she pleased him, he let her have the vibrations. When she didn't, it was an electric zap. Not enough to harm her, but it hurt like a son of a bitch. Every time he did it, he reminded her he was going easy on her and using one of the lower settings.

They must have been in the gym for two hours. She'd lost count of both the number of zaps and the number of orgasms she'd been subjected to. Lindsay's words from earlier about how she'd beg not to come anymore were ringing in her ears, and the day wasn't half over.

The session ended on the treadmill, as Brian ran her to the point of exhaustion. Somehow him using her body in the gym was even more degrading than if he'd thrown her down on the ground and systematically violated each hole.

He'd taken to torturing her with orgasms instead of electricity by the end, leaving the toy on the strongest setting even after she came. As she ran on the treadmill, she wasn't sure anymore if she was running toward or away from the constant stimulus.

Finally, moments before she thought she'd pass out, he told her to stop and handed her a bottle of water. She didn't say the words, but her eyes begged him to be done with her. She would have gladly consented to a rerun of the episode of her cleaning another woman's pleasure from his boots while he jerked off, just to stop the pain he'd heaped on her here.

Vivian was almost to the point where she'd beg him to. Almost to the point where she'd let him use her here in the gym in front of anyone who cared to watch, just to distract him from the one type of sadism he'd been allowed to visit upon her without restraint or a babysitter.

He laughed and shook his head, no doubt reading the defeat and desperation in her eyes. "If I could do it without getting in trouble, I'd ride you so hard in bed and in the dungeon, you'd beg to come back to the gym for more of this abuse. There is no reprieve with me. Eventually they'll let me play with you, and you'll find out."

She was too weak to hold herself up, but he didn't help her. He just let her crumple to the ground.

Brian walked away but came back a few moments later and shoved another glass of something in her face. "Drink this. Proteins. Nutrients. It'll replenish the stuff you just lost. Don't drink it too fast or you might get sick."

She sipped the chocolate-flavored shake.

"You may leave when you're able to leave. Or you can sit on the floor all day. I don't care which. I'll see you again the day after tomorrow. Tomorrow you have to rest to rebuild the muscles we tore down."

She managed a weak "Yes, Sir" before he walked away in search of his next victim.

# FIFTEEN

It was an hour before Vivian felt recovered enough to stand under her own steam and leave the gym. If she'd had the strength she would have run far from her sadistic personal trainer from hell, but all she could manage was a slow, painful walk.

She told herself every day couldn't be this bad. She'd get used to his special brand of torture. She'd build stronger endurance. But she knew he'd only push her farther, harder, faster.

The rest of the afternoon was spent poolside. Men she'd never met, but had seen in passing, came by one at a time to lie on the lounger next to her. None of them felt compelled to strike up conversation, and none of them physically touched her.

The impersonal nature of the visits were, in her mind, worse than if they'd fondled her or taken her back to their room for some kinky slap and tickle. They merely laid next to her and pressed the little button until she came while trying not to look like she was coming. That part may have amused them the most. The fact that she was still so ridiculously shy.

Many of the other girls didn't seem to suffer from that problem, if the situation could be judged by the woman being openly fingered by the side of the pool. Vivian shuddered, hoping that wasn't her future. Gabe had said it wouldn't be, and it seemed the woman got off on being on display.

As if she'd read Vivian's mind, the woman glanced over and winked, then tossed her head back and came with a moan.

Vivian closed her eyes and went back to trying not to look like she was aroused. Each of the men had paid her a visit by now and they were starting the rotation again. Some began fast and hard, some began slow and let it go on at that low vibration forever, waiting for a pleading look or whimper before escalating the intensity.

The dark-haired stranger lounging next to her, was one of the latter.

"You have no idea how much I want to touch you and find out just how wet you are after all the times we've made you come today."

She was startled and uncomfortable by the sudden conversation. Apparently they could talk to her; they just hadn't wanted to. That somehow made it worse. They'd wanted to use her like a toy, manipulate her like a rag doll, watch her come undone for their own personal amusement.

Vivian chose her words carefully. "Why can't you touch me, Sir?" She hoped that didn't sound like an invitation. As attractive and sun-kissed as he was, it was yet another person to make her feel like a whore in the ever-growing list.

"I think I could if you said I could. They don't want to introduce you to anything too fast. They don't want to spook you."

His eyes were intense, drinking her in, and suddenly she wanted to let him touch her. If he touched her, it could only be with her consent. It felt like power. A type of power she hadn't had since coming to the house.

She wanted to consent, to explore and experiment with this new reality. To see if she could want this on her own terms, without threat or coercion.

"Okay," she finally said.

"Okay? Give me more than that, little one. I want to hear you beg for it."

She glanced toward several girls splashing in the pool, and then the trainer with the wanton slut who had stripped down to nothing and was happily giving him a blow job right there in front of God and everybody.

Vivian turned back to the stranger, growing increasingly aroused. "Please Sir, I want you to find out how wet I am."

He slid his sunglasses over his eyes and leaned back, feigning disinterest. "Hmmm. I need a more specific invitation than that or I can't do it."

This was the devil. This was what temptation was. Gorgeous evil wrapped in a mask of innocence and consent. And she found herself falling to his seduction. She didn't know where the words came from, or where her sudden bravery or shamelessness had been hiding out all this time.

"Please Sir, I need your fingers inside me so you can feel for yourself what a filthy slut I am."

He grinned, and a little dimple appeared in his cheek. He turned toward her and slid the sunglasses up to perch on the top of his head. "Much better."

He scooted his lounger closer and shoved aside her gym shorts, panties, and the toy. One finger dipped inside her, and she moaned as it started to wriggle around.

"I'm very pleased," he said.

Vivian couldn't stop the rush of pleasure at those words. Even coming from a random stranger she didn't know from Adam. She pushed her hips against him, begging for more contact. "Please . . . "

"But people could see you," he said in a low, teasing voice. "Whatever will they think?"

"Fuck it, I don't care. Use me." While the vibrator had teased and pleasured her clit to the point she'd lost count, his finger moving inside her was what she wanted right now. Penetration. Invasive, violating penetration.

He chuckled and slipped another finger in, pounding faster and harder. Vivian's head lolled to the side as tiny tugs of pleasure pulled at her with each thrust.

"Come for me, little one. I want to watch you come from my fingers using you, not some battery-operated toy."

She needed no more than those words of encouragement. She came undone, writhing, moaning, whimpering. When it was over, he prodded at her lips to let her suck his fingers clean, and she enthusiastically complied, sated and grateful.

Then she looked up, embarrassed to find she *had* attracted an audience. Gabe and Lindsay stood directly over the lounger, and a few others had been drawn to the fringes to catch a glimpse of the show.

"Jake, leave," Lindsay said.

It was clear by now that Gabe, Lindsay, and Anton were the power players here. Everyone else appeared to answer to the three of them. She wasn't sure what the exact hierarchy was, but it was obvious they were at the top.

Jake, the man whose name she'd just learned *after* she'd come, shrugged and got up. He winked at her, then slid the sunglasses over his eyes and walked away.

Gabe turned to go back inside and Lindsay held out a hand to help Vivian up. She was still sore from the gym, but allowed the doctor to lead her to his room.

"Am I in trouble?" she asked when he'd closed the door.

He didn't answer. Instead he asked, "Did Jake force you?"

She looked at the ground. Suddenly feeling uncomfortable standing next to him, she dropped to her knees and kissed his shoes. "No, Sir."

His fingers threaded through her hair. "No, you aren't in trouble. You were told none of them were allowed to play with you, not that you weren't allowed to play with them. I think no one imagined you'd initiate something, especially this early. Tell me why you did it."

"He gave me a choice. I wanted to know what it would be like to freely submit."

"You made a choice every time you went back to Dome."

"That's not the same."

He nodded. "From now on, you are only to be with me, Gabe, or Anton unless we say otherwise."

The *unless we say otherwise* hung on the air, threatening Vivian with the potential of Brian. She wanted to ask if they'd ever let him touch her, but was afraid to hear the answer.

Instead she simply said, "Yes, Sir. I'm sorry. Are you disappointed in me?"

"No, Vivian. You weren't disobeying anyone. And I told you you'd lose all your inhibitions. This is progress."

Lindsay spent the rest of the day fucking her and fulfilling his promise of tiring her out on orgasms. It was as if he was training her body so it didn't know how to resist or close to pleasure. He wanted to wring every drop of it from her, and then when she thought she was wrung dry, he would start again, pushing her farther each time, until she began to internalize her own surrender and the power these men held over her body.

He ordered food for them, and it was served in the room. After she'd eaten, he went to work on her again, using her for his own pleasure, then demanding she give him hers as she orgasmed for him on demand. When they were both sated, he allowed her to sleep in the circle of his arms.

# SIXTEEN

Days turned into weeks, and the banshee finally died. With each day of pleasure and rigid rules and obedience, Vivian allowed another piece of herself to drift free. Gabe commented one day on the fact that she was the least punished girl they'd ever trained and how much it pleased him. The idea of their displeasure drove her even more strongly than the threat of punishment.

They molded and trained her body so well she could barely remember a time when she couldn't come or a time when she would have felt shame over it. Shame became an abstract concept, cloistered as she was in this place where the only shameful thing was being modest or disobedient.

She transformed into something she didn't recognize, but liked, even if someone from her old life would have told her she shouldn't. When she looked in the mirror on the rare occasions she had a free moment in her room, she saw a new confidence and peace had slipped over her features. The lines that had begun to form on her face softened as everything inside her relaxed.

At first she'd feared they would start sharing her with others, especially Brian. But the fear never came to fruition, despite his complaints that she'd been there long enough. She wasn't sure why, but Anton was possessive of her in a way he wasn't with the others. After awhile, the excuse that she'd been brought to the house too soon, wore thin. That couldn't be the real reason. Not anymore.

She'd come to think of herself as perhaps special to him because he seemed to go easier on her and protect her more than others. Vivian had convinced herself this favor she'd garnered was because of how deeply and completely she'd submitted to them.

Her training was split evenly among the three men, Anton deciding that she was becoming too attached to Gabe and Lindsay. As if adding himself back into the mix would solve anything. She was attached to all of them and hated waking every morning because she knew each day took her closer to the day she'd be sold.

She'd developed a fantasy that the three leaders of this house had become so charmed with her they'd never sell her. She'd remain in the house forever with them dominating and possessing her. One morning Anton stepped into the room and burst that fantasy bubble.

Vivian knew something important was about to happen because Gabe was nowhere in sight, and he always came in for their morning shower. She wiped the sleep from her eyes as the grogginess lifted. Everything felt surreal as she left the bed and crawled over to kiss his boots.

He stroked her hair. "Did you sleep well, flower?"

She kept her head down. "Yes, Sir."

"I have excellent news. Tomorrow morning you're going to have a master."

Everything in her seized up, then she started to cry. "Please, don't sell me. I don't want to go. I thought . . . " She shut her mouth to stop herself from spilling out her absurd fantasies.

"You thought we'd keep you? That you'd be the house pet?"

She shrugged, still not able to meet his eyes.

"You've been sold for half a million just as I said you would be. What could you possibly do to be worth that price if I let you stay?"

"Nothing, Sir." Whatever they wanted of her, they could get, free of charge.

All at once the room began to grow smaller. Her throat tightened; her breath came out in short bursts. Anton was crouched beside her an instant later, raising her chin. "Stop it."

"I can't help it."

"What is wrong with you? You've been lovely. Better than lovely. You've been a dream to train, much better than I ever expected. And now you're having a breakdown?"

She felt as if she were regressing back to the night she'd been brought to the house, suddenly needing to latch onto anything that would rescue her from this world and put her back someplace safe. "I want Michael. Please, if you don't want me, send me back to him. He'll pay you. Please."

Anton laughed. "He'd pay half a million dollars to get you back? After everything you've done in this house? After everything you've enjoyed? I have hours and hours of footage of you writhing around like a bitch in heat, taking cocks and toys in every available orifice. You want to go back to your husband after that? To your safe life where you play the little woman and get your nails done? Is that what you want?" His voice came out clipped, his accent causing words to blur together.

"Yes."

"Liar. What did we say about lying, Vivian? Do you wish to be punished on your last day with us?"

She shook her head. "No, Sir."

There were a thousand things she wanted to say, a thousand things she wanted to accuse him of. If the banshee were still with her, screaming and crying in indignation, she would have had a laundry list of grievances to assault him with.

She could have complained about how none of it was really her fault. There had been blackmail and coercion and later kidnapping. He'd led her into this spider's web. She'd had no choice, no hope.

But she could no longer give credence to those lies. The first day with Anton in Dome, when she'd spread her legs for him, she'd done it without much fuss or fighting because she needed to know if anyone could make her feel.

Anything.

She'd needed to remember what it felt like to surrender under the hands of another and feel pleasure. And he'd done that for her, over and over, while giving her the comforting lie that he'd tell her husband, that he was somehow forcing her to these clandestine meetings.

Maybe he would have told Michael. But her choice had always been to come back, to allow herself to slip further under Anton's control. She'd played with the fire and still wasn't sure if she'd gotten burned, or if the fire had reshaped her into something new like a phoenix rising from the flame.

Michael was safety, but what Anton promised her was peace. She just didn't want to leave.

When her tears had run their course and the room was silent again, he spoke. "Tomorrow, when you are sold, you will be placed in your collar. You will address him as *Master* when you meet him. Annette will walk you through the protocol. Do you understand?"

"Yes, Sir."

He left, Gabe came in, and the day went along like any other. Even on her last day she wasn't spared the gym where Brian let out all his sadism on her in the only way he was allowed. During their session he seemed pissed off.

He must have known she'd be leaving without him ever getting to dip his wick in her. She couldn't say she was very upset about that. She tried not to look smug as he pushed her on the treadmill.

Later Annette talked her through the events for the following day and how she was to behave and what she was to say.

That night all three of them used her. They took her into the large bathroom on the first floor with the Jacuzzi tub large enough to hold them all. They bathed her and fucked her, repeatedly. By the end of the night she was so well-used, she was a languid heap of pleasured nerve endings.

Each of them pressed a kiss to her cheek before leaving her to sleep. But she didn't sleep. She couldn't. She'd tried so hard that night to float away, to not experience any of it too strongly. Even though she'd come so many times she lost count, she'd tried to remain detached because the thought of never seeing any of them again, of going off to become the property of another, was too difficult.

Vivian laid awake, staring at the ceiling, tossing and turning until she finally couldn't stand it any longer and kicked the blankets off. They'd stopped chaining her to the wall at night because she never gave them reason to think they couldn't trust her.

She'd never explored the mansion after dark. She'd never felt the compulsion, and she'd been afraid of the consequences. Now, punishment didn't matter as much.

Please them or displease them, they'd decided to sell her.

Some rich, entitled man had watched videos of her fucking and being trained, had chosen her to belong to him and agreed to pay their price. They'd done the proper background checks, no doubt.

Anton would have gone to extra trouble to check out the buyer, ensuring he was safe, kind, and fair. As much as those things were possible in this situation. He would have made sure the buyer could give her what she needed.

The floor was cold on her feet as she slipped through the house. She crossed through the cafeteria and out to the breezeway. When Vivian got outside, she looked up at the stars and breathed in the fresh air. The pretty illusion of freedom.

The edge of the property line seemed to call to her. Lindsay had walked her out there one day, showing her where the bracelet would be set off, the point where she'd be considered a runaway. After that day she'd never come near the line.

But tonight she stood here, less than a foot from the spot that would wake the whole house. She sat in the grass, staring at the boundary. She knew she couldn't escape. That wasn't the point.

If she did it, they'd punish her. They'd believe she wasn't fit to be sold. How much time would that buy her?

The grass stirred and she jumped. Lindsay sat and pulled her against his chest. "Couldn't sleep?"

"No, Sir." She knew he heard the tears in her voice.

"Crossing that line wouldn't allow you to stay. It would only make us disappointed in you. I know you don't want to go. I don't want you to go, but the sale has gone through. Money has exchanged hands. It can't be undone, and even if it could, Anton wouldn't undo it."

They sat that way for a long time, until finally he stood and helped her to her feet. "Come. You can sleep in my room tonight."

Without a word she followed him up the sloping hills back to the side entrance, then through the enormous house and up to the second floor to his room at the end of the long, silent hallway. When they were behind the door, he pushed the button on the wall to turn the water on for the plants.

She collapsed into the bed, exhausted, and closed her eyes. His arm came around her, and she drifted to sleep while the rain came down.

*Vivian woke to the sounds* of arguing. Gabe and Lindsay. She looked back and forth between the two as if she were watching a ping pong tournament. Gabe was angry she hadn't been in her room. Cursing and heated words were exchanged, and then he grabbed an unresisting Vivian out of bed.

Lindsay slammed the bathroom door without a word or glance back. That was her goodbye to him. Then Gabe got her into the shower back in her room. His hands slid over her body, all cold business. She wanted to lash out at him, yell something about the fact that he'd wanted to have her in the shower, and now he wasn't taking advantage of their last moments together.

But she didn't. They'd trained her too well, and even now, she couldn't bring herself to rebel enough to make one of them disappointed in her during her last hours in the house. Gabe didn't try to have sex with her or even get a blow job out of the deal. He didn't allow her to wash him. He just cleaned and dried her off.

He went to the dresser drawer and tossed a corset, panties, and garter belt at her, along with some fuck-me pumps. "You're leaving with your master in this, today," he growled.

Then he, too, was gone.

Vivian stood, stunned. She was scared enough about what was about to happen and neither Gabe nor Lindsay could be bothered to get out of their heads and their own issues. An hour later Annette brought her breakfast and asked if she was okay.

It seemed to be a rhetorical question because when Vivian tried to get into a conversation with the other woman, she looked like a doe caught in headlights and made an excuse to leave.

Soon after, when her nerves were completely frazzled, her mouth was dry, and she thought she might faint or cry or scream or all three, Anton walked into the room. He looked like he didn't want to let her go either.

"Please, Sir . . . let me stay."

He shook his head. "I'm afraid that's not an option, flower. You'll understand in time." Then he said the words that made her blood run cold and her entire world pause.

"He's waiting for you in the showroom."

The showroom. Annette had told her about this. When they sold a slave, they presented her in a lovely room and paraded her around, making a grand show and ritual of changing ownership from the house to the buyer. Vivian guessed the buyer earned that much with the amount of money they forked over.

She crawled across the floor to Anton, pressed her lips against his boots, dripping tears onto them. "Please don't do this."

He bent and attached a collar around her neck. It wasn't leather like the one Annette wore; it was platinum with aquamarine stones set inside the band. It was the most gorgeous piece of jewelry Vivian had ever laid eyes on. It didn't even look like bondage-wear, at least not until a ring was attached around it, and then a leash. Anton unlocked the cuff from her wrist that kept her on the property.

She was looking down at her bare wrist and didn't see the blindfold until it covered her eyes. Annette had said this was the way things went, and yet she still wasn't prepared for how off-balance it made her, to not be able to steal a glance into the eyes of the man who bought her, to see if there was something human in him she could trust.

Anton jerked on her leash a little, and she knew she'd never see his face again. The trip down the hallway seemed to take forever. He let her walk until they got to the showroom because it was down one level.

When they arrived, Anton said, "down," and she dropped to her hands and knees. He led her across the plushly carpeted floor and stopped.

"May I present your slave, Vivian."

She groped in the darkness and bent to kiss the shoes of the stranger. "Master, this slut is yours," she said, sure she'd pass out and thankful that was all she had to say.

"If you have any trouble, you may bring her back for further training. We'll check in with you in a couple of weeks to make sure you're happy with your purchase."

Anton's footsteps receded softly over the carpet.

There was silence for a long time. She heard a glass being filled and muffled whispers. She knew the man who'd bought her was being served a drink, perhaps something to eat.

The truth of the latter was confirmed when his hand pressed a bit of food to her mouth. A strawberry. She opened and ate it while he ran a hand over her. After several minutes, he stood and tugged on her leash.

This was really happening. If the blindfold hadn't been over her eyes, she would have felt the edges of the room go dark anyway. Such was the level of her panic. When they got to the entryway of the mansion and the hard, marble floor, he gripped her gently by the elbows and brought her to stand. Then he led her the rest of the way outside.

The man helped her into the back of a car and joined her, then he tapped on the glass, and the driver started the engine. She felt the car lurch away, taking her to god knew where. He slipped off her panties, then his fingers were inside her.

In spite of the circumstances and her anxiety, her body fired up like the well-trained machine it was. Vivian was immediately wet and flushed, knowing she was dripping down his hand, that he would know what a horny little slut she was, even without yet seeing his face. He could look like a scruffy cave dweller, and it probably wouldn't matter.

His thumb flicked against her clit while his fingers pumped inside her, and she began to climb toward her orgasm in earnest. "Master, please," she gasped out. She'd had to fight to remember not to call him *Sir*, that this wasn't one of her trainers, though that was what she'd been fantasizing. The fantasy had been easy to engage in with the blindfold still shutting out the world and her new reality.

"Yes, come for me, Vivi."

She froze.

Michael. She reached to remove the scrap of black fabric from her eyes, her emotions so torn she didn't know what to think or do. The urge was strong to start yelling at him, screeching as the banshee rose from the dead to take her indignant revenge for this betrayal. Because it must have been planned. If he'd come to rescue her, he wouldn't have started fingering her like that in the car when she was still scared, not knowing who he was.

His free hand gripped her wrist hard before she could take off the blindfold. "I don't believe I gave you permission to do that. Come like I asked, or there will be consequences."

His hand was still grinding against her heat, harder, punishing the swollen nub he'd been expertly manipulating. Had he taken a class or had she really been that shut down before? Her stomach tightened in response to his words and the way he handled her. Then despite all her jumbled emotions, despite the relief of being back with him, loving him, hating him, wanting him, being repulsed by him, she came, dripping in the back seat of the limo.

Michael kissed her, and she opened to him. She melted against his body in post-orgasmic bliss, her mind still whirring over what he'd done. The audacity of it. The fucked-up evil of it. The fact that she was wetter than she remembered ever because of it. He ripped the blindfold off her face and they just stared at each other for a long moment.

They were on the main road now, the tinted windows blocking out the sunlight and protecting the world from their debauchery. The look he gave her was so heated, so savage, she had to look away.

Tears filled her eyes. "Michael, why . . . "

A hand cracked hard against her thigh. "Not Michael. Never Michael again. Master. And that's exactly why. Even with everything I've set in motion, you still can't believe it. You want to see me as your tame little husband. No more."

He held up a hand to stop her from speaking. She had a feeling if she pushed him, he'd put a gag in her mouth so he could say what he had to say. She was desperate for answers, and a little scared. What was this man capable of, and how had she never seen it? Had he just snapped one day? Even with his business tactics she never would have believed he'd take anything this far.

"We weren't happy, Vivi. We were dying in that sanitized little world we created. I wanted more. I wanted *this*."

He pulled her panties up, then pushed her onto her knees in front of him while he petted her hair. The display of power imbalance was not lost on her.

"Why didn't you just tell me? Why bring others into it?"

"Because it wouldn't be real. And even if it was, you wouldn't accept it. You wouldn't believe in it. Do you know what I'd have to do to you to make you truly understand your new place with me? I'd have to punish you so severely you'd always fear me. We've been so normal and vanilla our whole marriage that springing this on you now . . . you never would have accepted it."

"You could have tried. You could have given me a choice."

"You had a choice. You kept going back to Anton. You wanted the things he did to you. I saw the way your eyes lit up the few times I got angry with you and didn't let you push me around, but it didn't matter. You would have fought me. Anton, Gabe, and Lindsay are friends of mine. They offered to train you so I wouldn't have to break you myself."

She stared at his feet. "You're fucking crazy," she whispered

He sighed. "And you're planning your escape."

"Hell yes, I am."

"Lindsay warned me this might happen. Do not push me, Vivi. I love you, but don't think for one minute I'll tolerate you giving me an ounce less respect than you gave those men."

"Love. Do you even know what love is?"

"We'll deal with this when we get home."

When they arrived at the house, he had to drag her inside.

Michael led her down the hallway toward the basement. He retrieved a key and unlocked the door, then she was being pushed downstairs. Her eyes widened when she got to the bottom. He'd turned it into a dungeon.

"How long have you been working on this?" she asked.

"Months."

The level of premeditation shouldn't have shocked her, but it did. He removed the leash and took the little ring off. Now it looked like any other piece of expensive jewelry. "You will never remove this collar without my permission. Do you understand me?"

"Yes," she mumbled, still not meaning it.

"Yes, what?"

"Yes, Master."

He attached cuffs to her wrists, and then raised them over her head to attach to a sturdy metal hook in the ceiling.

She could feel his anger pulsing off him as he ripped her panties off and went to get a cane. The first whack made every nerve ending in her body light up and cringe away from him.

"Who do you belong to?"

She shook her head. "This is abuse. This is fucking abuse. You sick fucking bastard."

Michael moved to stand in front of her, his hand gripping her throat. She tried to avoid his eyes, didn't want him to see the lust in them. Didn't want to feel the lust at all.

"Look at me or I promise you will regret it. You know what I'm capable of now."

She turned her gaze to his, letting him have the full force of her hatred.

"Is this abuse, Vivi? Or is it abuse to just let you rot away and die like you were doing? Did you like that feeling? Do you want to live a lie with me while we both fucking rot away from the inside? Or do you want something real? TELL ME!"

"I can't . . . this is wrong."

"I watched the videos. I saw everything that went on with you and them. I saw how you surrendered. I saw the wanton, slutty way you behaved. I jerked off to it every night. This is in you. You'll give it to them, to strangers, but not your own goddamned husband?"

"They didn't betray me. They were bad to begin with. I thought you were better than that."

He wrapped his arms around her, burying his head in her neck. "Oh, I can be good. Submit to me and you'll never doubt it again, but you had to see what lengths I would go to. You are mine. You will acknowledge you are mine. I am your master, and if you don't learn it today, you'll go back to the house and be trained until you do learn it."

She wanted to give in. So badly. What he'd done was so wrong, but the throbbing between her legs hadn't stopped since he'd revealed himself in the limo. So who was the sick fuck? Him or her? Both of them? Who the fuck cared anymore?

She'd wanted the safety of Michael but the control of Anton. And now the reality slammed home that he could give her both. Was she really willing to throw it all away? For what? For pride? For some philosophical viewpoint on rights? For social acceptability?

The tears sprang from her eyes, wetting his suit.

"That's it, Vivi. Let it out. Who do you belong to?"

"You, Master." She felt the little surrender, the first small step to bonding with him, as she'd bonded with her trainers. Though this would be more, and that both thrilled and scared the hell out of her.

"Good girl," he cooed in her ear. His hand moved down to cup her sex. "Who does this belong to?"

"You, Master," she said, her voice stronger this time.

"From this point onward, your body's responses belong to me and whoever I share you with. Whether I want you to go for a week without coming or come every ten minutes, you'll do it because you're mine."

"Share?"

"We're going to be alone like this for about a month. When you've fully bonded to me, once a week I'll send you to the house to play. You are my slut, and you'll spread your legs for whoever I say. If I want to add more people to that list I will, and you'll gladly comply. Are we clear?"

"Yes, Master."

He chuckled at the breathy way her voice came out. "Such a dirty slut. I should have done this a long time ago."

"So you didn't really pay them?"

"I paid them to train you. They're running a business, and I don't mooch off my friends."

The silence stretched between them for several minutes. "Vivi, I'm giving you one freebie. I won't punish you because I understand why you're upset and why you feel you have to fight so hard. But don't believe I'll go easy on you. Forget our previous relationship. It doesn't exist. I am the man who bought you today. You're safe with me, but I won't let you use my love for you against me."

She sagged in the chains, making bargains with herself. She told herself she'd surrender to him for a week, maybe two and see how it went. She could always leave him. But even as she thought it, she knew she wouldn't go anywhere. She was only appeasing the newly risen banshee, shutting her up so she could quietly kill her again, this time forever.

He unlocked her wrists, rubbed them, then carried her upstairs. His fingers fumbled over the corset.

"Master?"

"Yes, pet?"

She flushed at the new endearment. "Did you pick this collar for me?" Her fingers grazed over the jeweled band.

"I did."

"Thank you. It's beautiful."

He nodded and guided her to the bed. "Tomorrow I'll lay out the rules. I also intend to do every filthy thing that was done at the house, and more. But today has been hard for you. I'm sorry you were so scared. I'll be gentle today."

"Please don't be gentle."

He smiled. "There's my little slut."

Michael bent her over the bed and took what was his. She writhed and moaned like a bitch in heat as he coaxed her body to obey.

"This was well worth the cost of training," he said.

Vivian should have been pissed at that, but the training came back to her as if today had been a glitch. She bucked underneath him, unsure if she was fighting to get away or fighting to get closer. Every thrust sent her soaring higher, wanting to give him more.

"Come, Vivi."

It had been six weeks since he'd last fucked her. The headboard of the bed thumped against the wall in rhythm to Michael's thrusts. She came for him, moaning his new name.

# EPILOGUE

*6 weeks ago . . .*

Michael sat at the card table at the club with Gabe, Anton, and Lindsay, the poker cards dealt.

"You're always so sour now," Gabe said.

Michael knew he was sulking, but he couldn't help it. He'd grown tired of Vivian acting like he was a villain for wanting to screw his own wife. The horrors. He wanted her, not his secretary, not the slutty waitress who kept bringing his drinks. Her.

"You never should have married that girl," Lindsay said, seeing through to the root of things. The doctor was far too perceptive for his own good. Always with his shrink hat on.

"That *girl,* is the woman I love," he ground out, irritated.

"But she doesn't give you what you need," Anton said, flinging his chips to the center of the table.

Michael tossed his chips in and fought back the urge to yell at his friends. He'd met Anton's slave one evening when Vivian thought he was at the gym. He'd watched her lovely submission, she way the word *Master* tripped off her lips, even with a stranger present. He'd grown hard watching the way she'd knelt at his friend's feet.

Anton had asked if Michael wanted to use her, that she'd be happy to oblige him. Looking into her eyes, she'd seemed excited and turned on by the idea. He'd refused the offer, knowing it would only make him more bitter on his return home.

He laid his cards on the table and curses filled the air as he pulled the chips toward himself. "I want what you have," he finally said. His eyes leveled on Anton.

"There is no way your wife will put up with you having a slave."

"She will if she's the slave."

All three of them looked at Michael as if he'd grown a third head, and perhaps he had. It took a few drinks and an hour to bring them over to his plan and orchestrate how each of them would play their role to train his wife.

"I won't do anything different from what I normally do," Anton said, "If I don't think she needs this, I'll let her go. I won't take a woman who isn't wired to submit and turn her into this. Not even for you."

Michael nodded, fighting back the eye roll. Anton fancied himself a civilized monster who played by a code of ethics that precluded him from taking a woman without deep needs to submit, using too brutal punishment, or selling them to anyone he hadn't properly checked out.

If Michael hadn't married Vivian, he'd probably be working in Anton's house of debauchery right now, taking innocents and molding them for a life of sexual servitude they'd been trained to enjoy.

*A few days later . . .*

"Honest opinion," Michael said into his cell phone when he knew Vivian had enough time to leave Lindsay's office in the city.

Lindsay sighed over the phone. "Honestly? I'm not sure. She's so tightly wound. I gave her Anton's card. He'll work it out from there."

A few hours later he called Anton. "Well?"

The man chuckled over the phone, then the richly accented voice said, "Oh, she's a submissive. She came for me like a rocket and I think forgot during that time that I'd closed off her escape. She didn't put up much of a fight."

Michael smirked. "What now?"

"Now, we wait. She'll be back, and when she's ready I'll take her to the house."

*A few days later . . .*

The four of them sat in the sauna at the club while Michael pumped Anton and Lindsay for more information.

"What happened exactly at the restaurant, Lindsay?"

"She's not ready yet. But I can see it in her eyes. We'll get there," he said.

"You need to leave town," Anton said.

"What? That wasn't part of the plan."

"I don't think she'll let herself go fully until she doesn't have to face you every night. Just take away her ability to pay me, and invent a business trip."

Michael took a deep breath and let it out on a sigh.

"It'll be worth it when we finish with her. Trust me."

*A few weeks later . . .*

Michael was in Mexico lying on a private beach, trying not to think about what was going on with Vivian when his cell rang. Anton's number flashed across the screen.

"Yes? Is she okay?"

"Calm down. She's fine. I just have to move the timetable up. I'm about to take her to the house."

His chest tightened and for a brief moment, he considered backing out. But he was too committed. If they stopped now, she'd be like an unfinished piece of art. And it would hurt her. She'd have to be put into therapy for shit he'd initiated. By this point it was more merciful to continue the conditioning.

"Why are you taking her so soon?"

"She's a loose cannon. I won't compromise my operation on this, Michael. I'm taking her to the house. Don't worry, it'll just be me, Gabe, and Lindsay. We'll take good care of her for you."

"I want to talk to her before she gets there."

"Call in thirty minutes. We'll be on the road."

*A few days later . . .*

Michael was livid. "I'm coming over there right now. I'll fucking kill that bastard!"

Anton's voice slid over the phone in that calming fashion that always somehow convinced Michael everything was okay. "Brian has been dealt with. He won't touch her that way again."

"He'd better not. It's one thing for you three. You're like brothers, and you know I don't mind sharing her with you. But I hate that fucker. I've hated him since college. I don't know why you employ him."

"Relax. Everything is fine."

"Is she okay?"

"She's fine. Gabe took care of her. She'll be ready for you in a few weeks."

*Today . . .*

Michael sat on the edge of the bed, stroking Vivian's hair as she slept. Her collar glinted off the light of the lamp. He'd known this would be difficult. Could he have trained her himself? Probably not. He wouldn't have had the stomach for it. And she never would have believed in it.

The cell phone vibrated in his pocket. He disentangled his limbs from Vivian's and moved into the hallway.

"Yes?"

"How is she?" It was Gabe.

"It was both easier and rougher than I expected. She seemed to submit to me, but there was a fight first."

The other man sighed loudly over the phone. "Don't let up on her. Don't let her get away with a single thing or you'll lose everything we did. I don't know why the fuck you didn't just come to the house as one of her trainers. It would have been a more controlled circumstance, instead of springing it on her like this."

Michael gave a non-committal grunt, and Gabe let the issue drop.

"Lindsay wants to know if you're bringing her back for visits."

"In about a month. I told her then she'd go to the house weekly."

"How did she feel about that?"

Michael scrubbed a hand through his hair, "She was trying to be nonchalant. I guess she doesn't want me to be jealous, but I could tell she's excited."

He talked to Gabe for a few more minutes and then disconnected the call. His mind went back to the other man's accusation about why he'd handled things in the end as he had.

They would never understand. Michael needed one moment with Vivian where she didn't have anger or assumptions about him, where she was his slave and he was her master without any other layers of bullshit.

When Anton had brought her to him and she'd knelt at his feet and offered herself to him as his property, when she hadn't known it was him, it was honest. Her fear, her surrender, everything.

The moment the blindfold came off, things got complicated, as he'd known they would. They would eventually get back to that place where she understood herself as his slave and not his wife pretending to be his slave. But either way, he would always have that one moment.

Where it was real.

It made the entire fucked-up thing worth doing all over again.

CPSIA information can be obtained
at www.ICGtesting.com
Printed in the USA
LVHW091943180719
624553LV00001B/2/P